CANOE JOURNEY

LIFE'S JOURNEY

CANOE JOURNEY
LIFE'S JOURNEY

A Life Skills Manual for Native Adolescents

Developed by

Journeys of the Circle Project for Urban Native Adolescents, Seattle Indian Health Board,
and
Addictive Behaviors Research Center, Department of Psychology,
University of Washington, Seattle, Washington

Compiled and edited by

June La Marr, Ph.D., and G. Alan Marlatt, Ph.D.

With contributions and review by the Project Team:

Seattle Indian Health Board
Ralph Forquera
Rebecca Corpuz
Steve Gallion
Crystal Tetrick
Al Sweeten

Addictive Behaviors Research Center
G. Alan Marlatt
Mary Larimer
Pat D. Mail
Lisa Thomas
Lillian Huang Cummings
Elizabeth Helen Hawkins
Sandra Radin
Karen Chan
Tammy Abab

With a special contribution from Tulalip Tribes elder Della Hill

Funding for this project was provided by a
National Institute on Alcohol Abuse and Alcoholism grant, RO1 AA12321

HAZELDEN

Hazelden
Center City, Minnesota 55012-0176

1-800-328-0094
1-651-213-4590 (Fax)
www.hazelden.org

The passage on pages 20–21 is reprinted from *Black Elk Speaks: Being the Life Story of a Holy Man of the Oglala Sioux* by John G. Neihardt by permission of the University of Nebraska Press. Copyright © 1932, 1959, 1972 by John G. Neihardt. © 1961 by the John G. Neihardt Trust. © 2000 by the University of Nebraska Press.

To purchase additional copies of this book, log on to www.hazelden.org/bookstore or call 1-800-328-9000 for more information.

Cover design by David Spohn
Interior design and typesetting by Kinne Design
Interior illustrations by Kari Lehr

CONTENTS

ACKNOWLEDGMENTS

This life skills intervention curriculum was developed over three years as a part of the Journeys of the Circle Project. The project developed out of concern for urban Native American adolescent youth, who are believed to be at higher risk for alcohol and substance abuse than youth of other ethnic groups in similar socioeconomic circumstances. The Seattle Indian Health Board (SIHB) found that a youth activities program was successful in engaging at-risk Native youth while providing opportunities to access health care services and substance abuse treatment programs. Lisa Thomas, a University of Washington Native psychology doctoral student, initiated discussions to explore effective strategies for intervening with at-risk Native adolescents. These discussions resulted in the collaboration of the SIHB and the Addictive Behaviors Research Center, Department of Psychology, University of Washington. The intent of this life skills curriculum is to provide Native youth with the opportunity to develop skills to help them make choices that motivate positive actions while avoiding the hazards of alcohol, tobacco, and other drugs.

No project of this magnitude is accomplished without the participation of many individuals. In this case, people from two programs worked together to develop *Canoe Journey—Life's Journey*. We apologize if we have missed identifying some of the people who made specific contributions. Our thanks go to those individuals who were instrumental in creating the idea, moving it forward, guiding it, recruiting adolescent participants, and performing the myriad of other tasks required to develop such a guide. In particular, special thanks are extended to the SIHB leadership, Ralph Forquera, Rebecca Corpuz, Crystal Tetrick and Al Sweeten, who supported the project and provided valuable feedback and direction. Additional appreciation goes to the SIHB staff who worked with the adolescents: Chris Chastain, Catherine Billiot, Truth Griffeth, Hazel Moraleja, Rita Walters, and Daisy Mazique. Special thanks are extended to Steve Gallion, who was the SIHB project director for more than two years. We thank Steve for believing in and supporting this project from start to finish.

The entire research and clinical team wishes to express thanks and appreciation to the Indian adolescents who participated in the first and second

Duplicating this page is illegal. Do not copy without publisher's written permission.

vii

interventions. They provided candid critiques and valuable insights into both the structure and content of the manual.

As the manual was being developed, Della Hill, a Tulalip Tribes elder, provided valuable information related to how a canoe journey is conducted. She also shared her experiences in participating in the canoe journeys over the past several years. We thank Della for sharing her perspective on this special cultural tradition. Lastly, we deeply appreciate her sharing of the remarkable story about the Orca whales. This story makes it clear why Pacific Northwest peoples see the canoe journey as a spiritual experience.

Several project staff members wrote drafts of various chapters, reviewed the material for accuracy and psychological appropriateness, and read versions for clarity, consistency, and accuracy. Ty Lostutter, Jessica Cronce, James Bruder, and Kelly Burns provided administrative assistance, support, and coordination throughout the project. We thank them for taking care of the very important but often overlooked "little stuff" that kept the team going.

Pat Mail, Ph.D., provided excellent material in the introduction on adapting the program for a variety of settings, including tribal adaptations, and made concrete suggestions on expanding or condensing the material. Also in the introduction, Lillian Huang Cummings, Ph.D., provided much-needed information on bicultural skills and approaches for adolescents and how this curriculum can enhance them.

Our deep appreciation is also extended to the Northwest Coast Natives who, in their wisdom, encouraged the resurrection of the modern-day Canoe Family. The challenge, hard work, pride, and spirituality in contemporary canoe journeys along the Washington and Canadian Pacific waterways have provided Native youth with positive activities, a traditional education, and direct experience with decision making, team building, intergenerational communication, physical and mental fitness, and a new sense of identity that will help them survive in two (or more) cultural domains. For their vision and creative work, we extend our heartfelt thanks.

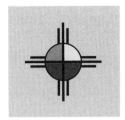

Introduction to the Curriculum

Canoe Journey—Life's Journey is an eight-session life skills curriculum that provides Native youth with the opportunity to develop skills that help them make positive choices in their lives while avoiding the hazards of alcohol, tobacco, and other drugs. The program emphasizes Native cultural traditions, with a canoe journey offering a metaphor for life's journey. The material is presented in a culturally appropriate manner. Two facilitators are ideal, especially for a large group, but one is sufficient.

The overall goal is to provide tools to cope successfully with life challenges and risks, and to enhance participants' views of the value of a clean and sober lifestyle. Participants also have opportunities to discover more about the Medicine Wheel, a traditional Native symbol, and how to incorporate it into daily living. Throughout the program, participants discuss the dangers of alcohol/drug use and how it compromises personal values. In the eight sessions, these dialogues are linked with positive topics including self-awareness, communities, goal setting and problem solving, communication, handling emotions, and strengthening body and spirit. Session-specific learner outcomes can be found at the beginning of each session.

The Origins of *Canoe Journey—Life's Journey*

Over a period of several years starting in 2000, a team of researchers from the University of Washington has worked with the Seattle Indian Health Board to develop a substance abuse prevention program that addresses the needs of urban Native youth in ways that are culturally congruent with the urban community and based on empirically validated principles. The project, named Journeys of the Circle, began with a series of focus groups with these young people. Soon a metaphor took shape, based on a cultural experience unique to Northwest Coastal tribes: the traditional Canoe Journey, whose participants form a "Canoe Family" that works closely together. This shared enterprise became the metaphor for the curriculum as it developed. Community elders were consulted on the project.

The metaphor is universal, although it is rooted in a particular region. The early Pacific Northwest Coast people preferred water travel to any other means of transportation. In recent years, the tradition has been revived: it is designed to strengthen Native identity, involve community members, and provide a drug- and alcohol-free environment. Early on, canoe clubs were formed for adolescents, but designed to accommodate and include families, and eventually the entire community.

Curriculum Features

Canoe Journey—Life's Journey is an eight-session program that provides life skills to adolescents ages thirteen through nineteen.

Organization

These eight sessions are organized around related topic areas, allowing a cyclic learning experience. Although one to two hours per session is typical, flexible timing is recommended. Session lengths should be determined by the interests of the adolescents: if they start talking about a particular topic, conversation should flow until it is complete. The curriculum is specifically designed for easy review: if something is learned from one part of the session, the leader can return to it when another concept is learned. This in turn creates a link between past concepts and current concepts.

Canoe Journey—Life's Journey utilizes group discussions, storytelling, role-plays, and handouts. In the facilitator guidebook, each session begins with an overview of its purpose, intended learner outcomes, and materials and preparation needed. A detailed outline then shows the actual content of the session, including dialogue starters and cues to distribute handouts. Reproducible handouts are included with each session in the guidebook; they are also provided on a CD-ROM.

The Medicine Wheel

This traditional Native symbol is used throughout the program as a metaphorical tool for seeking balance and wholeness. The medicine wheel is made up of four quadrants, each representing one of the four cardinal directions, as on a compass. As a whole, the program addresses four directions of human growth: mental skills, emotional coping skills, physical skills, and spiritual growth. Group didactics, discussion, role-playing, and handouts are used to train youth in goal setting, decision making, effective communication, coping with negative emotions, protecting the physical body, and enhancing spiritual values.

While the medicine wheel—or some rendition of it—is used by most tribes, some youth have little experience with it and will need to know more about it.

Youth from culturally traditional families are more likely to respond to it right away, but all participants can benefit from applying it in their daily lives.

Approaches to Facilitation

Two co-facilitators are ideal, especially for a larger group. However, when this is not possible, one facilitator is certainly enough.

Regardless of the number, facilitators review the session information beforehand so they can present it naturally, rather than reciting it verbatim. Because participants will be involved through role-plays, practice of skills, and reflective journal writing, leaders should create a sense of trust and safety, especially in the first session. Creating ground rules together helps in this process (outlined in session 1).

When talking about drug and alcohol abuse, leaders are respectful of all participants, keeping in mind their varied backgrounds and encouraging a variety of viewpoints. Some participants may have experimented with alcohol and/or drugs previously, or may be current users, while some have never experienced drug or alcohol use. They also may have family members and friends who are substance abusers.

Settings and Audience

Canoe Journey—Life's Journey was designed as a life skills intervention curriculum for Native American adolescents. Because of the versatility of the material, it can be used in a variety of settings, including schools, community programs, alcohol/drug treatment programs, and juvenile delinquency programs. Although it was developed specifically for urban Indian youth in Seattle, it is not tribe specific and can be used with any Native American population.

As a result of its Pacific Northwest origins, the program incorporates the canoe journey metaphor throughout. In other geographic and cultural regions, local stories, myths, and resources can be used to adapt the curriculum (see page 4). It can be customized for implementation in individual community settings as long as it is done in a culturally sensitive manner. Indeed, participants need not be of Native background. It can also easily be used with youth of other ethnic groups in similar socioeconomic circumstances; groups with varied ethnic backgrounds are common. The concepts are far reaching.

Evaluation

At the end of the program, efforts should be made to have participants evaluate the experience. Facilitators can devise some simple questions regarding the impact of the sessions, and ideas for enhancing the experience. Sample questions might include:

• Did the facilitators seem to understand the content?

- What kind of activities did you enjoy the most and why?
- What kind of activities did you enjoy the least and why?
- Were the role-plays helpful when learning new concepts and material?

These comments should be collected and compiled for training staff for future sessions.

Adapting the Curriculum

Canoe Journey—Life's Journey is an adaptable program. It can be revised for particular settings: it might be used as a traditional classroom course, a community-based intervention, a series of instructional periods in a summer day or residential camp for Native youth, or for individual or small-group counseling situations. It may be altered for various time frames, either lengthened or shortened. Although its concepts are universal, it can be adapted for various tribal groups as well. Some common questions on adaptations are addressed here.

Is the program designed only for group settings?
Although the facilitator guide assumes a group setting, the program is easily adapted for use in individual counseling sessions. In this instance, only one facilitator would be needed. One-on-one conversations will take the place of group discussions; little revision is needed.

Can it be used as a counseling tool?
In small therapeutic groups, those sessions that emphasize self-awareness, goal setting, and decision making can be used effectively. Discussions of drug use, the physiological and psychological effects of such use, and a range of consequences resulting from use should also be discussed.

When used as a counseling tool, the presentation can be made as though the sessions are part of a short course on behaviors and life skills, with emphasis on the consequences of choices.

I have plenty of time. What is the best way to expand the sessions?
When you are free to expand the sessions, consider the following strategies:

- If participants are willing, increase discussion times, and take care to involve everyone in them.
- When available and appropriate to the sessions, show a short video that focuses on the topic discussed.
- Introduce or expand role-playing as skills are learned. Role-plays are creative and effective learning tools.
- Revisit the "Who Am I?" exercise from session 2. Using the Medicine

Wheel concept to describe the four "elements of self," post some samples of fictitious adolescents. Have students talk about their characteristics and the type of behavior one might expect from an overemphasis on the physical, mental, emotional, or spiritual component.

- In addition to completing the Medicine Wheel at the end of each session, the participants may journal, using the handout as a starting point, recording what they learned or other impressions.

An example of a successful expansion adaptation: An eight-week summer day camp augmented *Canoe Journey—Life's Journey* with other youth activities that reinforced the sessions' lessons. The eight sessions were presented weekly in 60- to 90-minute periods on Tuesdays. On Wednesday afternoons a group activity was presented that augmented or reinforced the focus of the Tuesday session. Later, a Friday or Saturday activity followed for additional play plus lesson emphasis. Activities were structured to utilize such concepts as teamwork, communication, and building self-efficacy.

This same approach could be developed for school days: Sessions could be held either in class or as an after-class period, followed by a weekend activity for the participating youth.

I'm short on time. What is the best way to condense the sessions?
There are options. Some settings, such as after-school classes, might require condensing the program. Or if it is administered during a small group or several individual counseling sessions as an intervention tool, quicker presentation and discussion may be required. In all cases, the facilitator must make decisions about collapsing content, de-emphasizing certain aspects of a session, or taking other steps to revise or reduce the presentation time without omitting important content.

Consider the following strategies:

- Combine and collapse session 2 with session 3. Sessions 4 and 5 may also be combined if needed.

- Identify each session's key concept and use just one main idea to teach the concept.

- Delay the journal writing (usually prompted by handouts) until the end of the entire curriculum. Or skip the journaling component altogether.

- Leave the Medicine Wheel exercises out of the body of each session, but retain the "What Did You Learn?" exercise at the end of each session (it also contains the Medicine Wheel).

- Use the handouts as the focus of each session.

Tribal Adaptations

Various tribal groups may want to adapt the curriculum to be more culturally congruent with their own traditions and stories. As this intervention focuses on journey by canoe, a specific Pacific Northwest tradition, it is likely that the canoe as a metaphor for life skills may not be appropriate for a Plains or Southwestern tribe.

For urban youth, a more generic pan-Indian approach may be appropriate. This is especially true when people know themselves to be Indian but cannot trace their ancestry due to foster placement or adoption. However, certain Indian ceremonialism and spiritual experiences are widely recognized and employed, even in communities where they are not indigenous. These include the wide use of the sweat lodge for educational, counseling, and spiritual practices[1] and the increase of drumming circles in treatment centers and for recreational purposes.

Canoe Journey—Life's Journey was developed in the Pacific Northwest where there is an abundance of water and dense forests. The canoe was the primary means of transportation before rail and road. Thus, the journey taken by curriculum participants employs the canoe as a metaphor for life's journey and the skills needed to interact with our traveling companions—the people in our life journey.

The Medicine Wheel symbolism is much broader than the immediate culture area, being widely recognized and employed by several tribal cultures. There are different versions of the Medicine Wheel. Communities may choose to use a more local version of the Medicine Wheel. The circle represented by the Medicine Wheel may also be known as a healing circle, a sacred circle, or some other name. The importance is the emphasis on the continuum of life, a sacredness in the lessons to be learned from the wheel, and the sense of balance achieved in the quadrants of the wheel.

Tribes wishing to adapt the curriculum should consider some of the following:

- If a Medicine Wheel or some other sacred circle was not traditional in a particular tribe, what symbols were used to represent balance, the cycle of life, and a representation of the larger environment within which the participants live?

- For a given tribe, what are its journey stories? Often these tell of a spiritual journey in which the traveler becomes a better and wiser person.

---

1. Hall, R.L. (1985). "Distribution of the sweat lodge in alcohol treatment programs." *Current Anthropology*, 26(1), 134–135.

- What was the prehistoric or traditional mode of travel in a tribe, village, or region? Was it by horse, foot, dog and travois, dugout canoe, bark-sided canoes, dog-powered sleds? Consider the metaphors suggested by those modes of transport.

- What different roles—dictated by factors such as age and gender—might be involved in such a traditional journey?

- How can the information here help lay the foundation for later interpersonal and decision-making skills required to be a positive member of the community?

An Evidence-Based Program

Canoe Journey—Life's Journey was developed over three years as a part of the Seattle Indian Health Board's Journeys of the Circle Project, involving University of Washington researchers. The project developed out of concern for urban Native American adolescent youth, who are believed to be at higher risk for alcohol and substance abuse than other youth in similar circumstances.

The program's developers applied best-practice approaches to their work, looking to the Substance Abuse and Mental Health Services Administration (SAMHSA), a federal agency, for guideposts. These included similar strategies for model prevention programs outlined by the Division of Knowledge Development and Evaluation at SAMHSA's Center for Substance Abuse Prevention. SAMHSA suggests six approaches that can be used alone or in combination:

1. information dissemination
2. prevention education
3. alternatives
4. problem identification and referral
5. community-based process
6. an environmental approach

The program was developed specifically to incorporate these best-practice approaches and strategies. The two publications listed on the next page include evaluations of the original *Canoe Journey—Life's Journey* project, conducted at the Seattle Indian Health Board and funded by the National Institute on Alcohol Abuse and Alcoholism (NIAAA).

- "Preventing Substance Abuse in American Indian and Alaska Native Youth: Promising Strategies for Healthier Communities" by E.H. Hawkins, L.H. Cummins, and G.A. Marlatt (2004). *Psychological Bulletin,* 130(2), 304–323. This article includes a positive review of *Canoe Journey—Life's Journey,* among other prevention programs. ***Abstract:*** Substance abuse has had profoundly devastating effects on the health and well-being of American Indians and Alaska Natives. A wide variety of intervention methods has been used to prevent or stem the development of alcohol and drug problems in Indian youth, but there is little empirical research evaluating these efforts. This article is an overview of the published literature on substance use prevention among Indian adolescents, providing background epidemiological information, a review of programs developed specifically for Indian adolescents, and recommendations for the most promising prevention strategies currently in practice.[2]

- "Journeys of the Circle: A Culturally Congruent Life Skills Intervention for Adolescent Indian Drinking" by G.A. Marlatt et al. (2003). *Alcoholism: Clinical and Experimental Research,* 27, 1–3. This article notes that preliminary research results regarding *Canoe Journey—Life's Journey* show a positive trend, most notably growth of self-efficacy, in resistance to alcohol and drug use in certain settings. ***Abstract:*** There has been an increasing call for and development of culturally appropriate substance prevention/intervention for ethnic minorities in schools and communities, especially among reservation and in urban American Indian and Alaska Native (ALAN) communities. Past attempts to intervene in and reduce misuse of alcohol and other drugs have not had great success. The Journey of the Circle Project utilized innovative programs with a strong emphasis on historic cultural traditions.[3]

---

2. Abstract from Hawkins, E.H., Cummins, L.H., and Marlatt, G.A. (2004), "Preventing substance abuse in American Indian and Alaska Native Youth: Promising strategies for healthier communities," *Psychological Bulletin,* 130(2), 304–323. Copyright © 2004 by the American Psychological Association. Reproduced with permission. For information on how to obtain the full text to this article, please visit http://www.apa.org/psycarticles.

3. Abstract from Marlatt, G.A. et al. (2003), "Journeys of the Circle: A culturally congruent life skills intervention for adolescent Indian drinking," *Alcoholism: Clinical and Experimental Research,* 27, 1–3. Reproduced with permission of Blackwell Publishing.

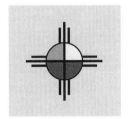

Bicultural Skills

In today's world, ethnic minority youth may often grow up identifying with more than one culture. While these adolescents might identify more or less with their ethnic minority culture, it is very likely that they will encounter and have to learn to function within mainstream American culture as well. *Bicultural competence* has been defined as the ability to draw strengths from both one's native culture and the majority culture. This ability seems to be more and more important as today's youth are constantly trying to navigate multiple cultural worlds, including family, community, school, and sometimes work. Developing certain skills that enhance bicultural competence may help our youth keep to the right path while navigating these diverse worlds.

Helping Native youth to become more bicultural may improve their overall mental, spiritual, physical, and emotional health by providing them with connection to their two cultures in each of these domains. The six dimensions of bicultural competence demonstrate how youth can work on these mental, spiritual, physical and emotional connections. These six dimensions are discussed here.

First dimension: Knowledge of cultural beliefs and values.

This has been defined as "the degree to which someone is aware of and knowledgeable about the history, institutions, rituals, and everyday practices of a given culture."[1] The more that youth know about both their Native and the majority cultures, the more they will understand how to fit and function well in both of these worlds. This knowledge brings us to the second dimension.

Second dimension: A more positive attitude toward both the Native and majority cultures.

Because youth will likely be interacting with both cultural groups, it may be helpful for them to feel positive about both cultures. This is not meant to

---

1. Definitions here are from LaFramboise, T., Coleman, H. L. K., and Gerton, J., "Psychological impact of biculturalism: Evidence and theory," *Psychological Bulletin* 115 (1993), 395–412.

Duplicating this page is illegal. Do not copy without publisher's written permission.

9

encourage adolescents to see the two groups as the same; in contrast, it can help them to see the unique benefits of each culture.

Third dimension: Bicultural efficacy.

This has been defined as "confidence that one can live effectively, and in a satisfying manner, within two groups without compromising one's sense of cultural identity." Bicultural efficacy will help youth maintain their own cultural identity while at the same time allowing them to develop positive interpersonal relationships in both cultures. Having friends and role models from two cultures will also improve their communication ability.

Fourth dimension: A diverse social network.

This will give adolescents a variety of sources of social support, which is often very helpful to them during these years of change and development.

Fifth dimension: Communication ability.

If youth can learn to communicate effectively, both verbally and nonverbally, in both cultures, they will feel more comfortable in their interactions in general. This sense of being heard and understood can contribute a great deal to their self-confidence.

Sixth dimension: Groundedness.

It may seem that living between two cultures may make youth feel confused and less confident in their sense of self. While it is true that living in two cultures can be stressful, when adolescents know about their own and the majority culture and when they feel positive, communicate effectively, fulfill roles, and establish friendships in both cultures, they may actually have increased self-confidence. This ability to have success and find support in both worlds can improve their overall health and well-being and in this way contribute to a greater sense of groundedness.

Role repertoire is "the range of culturally or situationally appropriate behaviors or roles an individual has developed." Individuals who are bicultural have the ability to be flexible in their roles and therefore can respond easily to the demands of both cultural environments.

Throughout *Canoe Journey—Life's Journey*, facilitators are reminded to recall Native values and worldview when teaching the various skill sets. Be aware that the way certain skills are used may be more or less appropriate, depending on the cultural context the youth is working in. For example, expressing assertiveness in an appropriate way might be done differently at home or in their Native culture than it would be done at work or in the majority culture. We suggest the following to help incorporate bicultural competence into *Canoe Journey—Life's Journey*.

Awareness of Cultural Values. Look through *Canoe Journey—Life's Journey* with an eye toward how different cultural values might influence the development of the various skills taught. It may be helpful to do this along with other facilitators before you start. Think about values such as collectivism. How might an emphasis on the group over the individual affect the usefulness of the material? How easily can participants incorporate it into their different cultural worlds?

Discussion of Differences. Throughout the curriculum, talk with the youth about how their use of these skills might vary depending on the context they are in. How might they use these skills differently in different settings such as home, school, work, and among friends? How would their family or friends respond if they started using these skills?

Discussion of Similarities. It can also be helpful to talk with youth about where they may see common ground; some skills may work well in both cultural worlds and therefore may be particularly useful.

Model Bicultural Competence. When discussing how cultural values might influence various situations, help youth to see both the benefits of and possible difficulties associated with those values. For example, if a culture emphasizes the importance of being nonconfrontational, youth may see that approach as less valuable in the context of a culture where assertiveness is expected and often necessary. In this situation, it may be helpful to talk with youth about the possible benefits of being nonconfrontational and brainstorm situations where this approach might help them or hurt them.

Duplicating this page is illegal. Do not copy without publisher's written permission.

11

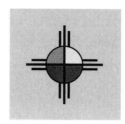

Notes on Cultural Sensitivity

Facilitators may find that these tips help bring out the best in participants and maximize the benefits of the program.

- Have knowledge of Native American culture, traditions, values, family and child-rearing practices, and so on. If a facilitator is non-Native, seek out and study materials on Native Americans; see this book's "Resources" section.

- Have knowledge of your region's Native community, its history, its customs, its roles (such as tribal officials, elders, and religious leaders), and its natural support systems (such as extended family, spiritual leaders, and religious and social functions). Tribal communities can usually offer some historical and cultural resources; some have cultural resource programs that also provide this type of information. Resources can also be found at local libraries. Participate in community gatherings, "culture nights," and so on.

- Have knowledge of the importance of the family and extended family. Your participants are likely to come from varying kinds of households: single-parent families, foster parent households, or families headed by other relatives such as aunts, uncles, or grandparents. Be sensitive to this in your choice of language and examples.

- Be aware that Native American families operate on varying levels of acculturation, which will affect response to interventions. Urban and rural Native families have varying levels of exposure to mainstream society: urban families are exposed constantly to the mainstream culture while rural families may have much less exposure.

- Have knowledge of community resources for mental health and substance abuse prevention, especially groups with Native American leaders and Native and non-Native service providers who are supportive of Native American individuals.

- Keep in mind that many participants may be reserved and quiet. However, this does not mean that they are not listening.

12

- Avoid making stereotypical assumptions; instead, ask questions.

- Be willing to share yourself. This is critical in developing rapport. If you don't want to share something about yourself, why should they be willing to share? Sharing could involve relevant personal experiences, tribal identity, and Native beliefs and values.

- Allow ample time for relationship building: humor, small talk, storytelling, and so on.

- Establish credibility and trustworthiness through genuine concern and respect. Participants are not likely to be impressed with education and degrees.

- Use active listening: reflecting, clarifying, restating, summarizing, and empathizing.

- Avoid confrontation, pressure, and manipulation; these tend to be ineffective.

- Be aware that the tradition of gift giving is deeply ingrained and should be respected and appreciated. Gifts are typically small and symbolic in nature.

Duplicating this page is illegal. Do not copy without publisher's written permission.

13

Preparation Tips for Facilitators

Use these tips to prepare for the program as a whole. Preparation reminders are found at the beginning of each session.

Room arrangement: Arrange seats to include every participant equally.

Handouts: Each session includes several handouts for use during the session. You can photocopy them from this guide; they appear after each session outline. Or you can print them from the CD-ROM (if using a color printer, decorative elements will appear in color). Note that some handouts are two pages long. Three-hole punch them if binders are used.

Binders or folders for handouts (recommended): Provide a binder or three-clasp folder to each student. For confidentiality, collect the binders at the end of each session and keep them in a locked cabinet. At the end of the whole *Canoe Journey—Life's Journey* program, participants can take them home.

Reading difficulties: Notice who might have trouble reading the handouts, and find a way to help without making it obvious. If possible, assess each participant individually in advance so you can anticipate their needs and ability to read aloud.

Breaks: Let participants know about breaks for snacks and using restrooms.

Prompting discussion: Spark conversation with your own questions and observations. If participants are quiet, try to guess out loud what they are thinking; they will correct you if you are off the mark. Two facilitators may find it easier to get the ball rolling; a solo facilitator may need extra creativity.

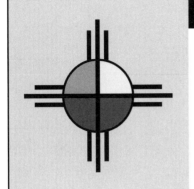

The Medicine Wheel and the Canoe Journey

METAPHORS TO LIVE BY

Purpose of Session 1

In this session, participants get to know each other and begin to learn skills to help them cope with life's problems and lead happier and healthier lifestyles. The Medicine Wheel becomes a tool to achieve a more satisfying, balanced life. Alcohol and drug use comes into focus as adolescents learn about obstacles that might disrupt a smooth canoe journey—and life journey.

Learner Outcomes

By the end of this session, participants will be able to:

- describe how the ideas and practices of a canoe journey can be applied to life's journey

- identify what the four directions of the Medicine Wheel (North, South, East, and West) can teach us about ourselves

- use their skills in order to provide a smoother canoe journey

- identify the physical effects of alcohol on the body

- identify the symptoms of alcohol abuse

Materials Needed

- ☐ flip chart, white board, or chalk board
- ☐ markers or chalk
- ☐ poster board
- ☐ masking tape
- ☐ handout 1.1, *Medicine Wheel Significance*
- ☐ handout 1.2, *Canoe Journey—Life's Journey*
- ☐ handout 1.3, *Native American Beliefs*
- ☐ handout 1.4, *Skills for Life's Journey*
- ☐ handout 1.5, *What Do You Know About Alcohol Use?*
- ☐ handout 1.6, *Physical Effects of Alcohol*
- ☐ handout 1.7, *Alcohol Use/Abuse*
- ☐ handout 1.8, *What Did You Learn?*

Preparation Needed

1. Read session 1 in its entirety to become familiar with it.

2. Reflect on the three stories found in this session: Black Elk's story, the Elder's story, and the Whale story. Ideally, be ready to tell them by heart, or you may read them aloud if you prefer.

3. Optional: Provide each student with a binder or three-clasp paper folder to hold all handouts. At the first session, have students write their names on them. They will turn in the binders at the end of each session. For confidentiality, keep them in a locked cabinet between sessions.

4. Photocopy all handouts and hole-punch if needed. Handouts appear in this book after each session outline; they can also be printed from the CD-ROM (if using a color printer, decorative elements will appear in color). During the session, distribute them one by one as prompted.

5. Arrange the room so that each participant can be included in the conversation.

6. Bring a piece of poster board so you can list the ground rules during session 1. Before each session, post these rules where everyone can see them.

Ground Rules

To open this session, the leaders introduce *Canoe Journey—Life's Journey* and participants establish some ground rules to create a safe learning environment. The ground rules should apply to any setting and can vary somewhat depending upon class size.

> ▶ **Facilitator Tip**
> Read the material beforehand and become familiar with it. Then, when talking to the class, you can paraphrase it in words that are natural to you. Note: some passages should be read aloud exactly as written—that text is in **bold italics**.

> ▶ **Facilitator Tip**
> Ideally, two facilitators will conduct each session. If this is not possible, as a solo facilitator, you will lead all aspects of discussion.

Introduce yourself and the co-facilitator (if applicable), then have all participants introduce themselves in turn.

> ▶ **Facilitator Tip**
> Your self-introduction might be the participants' first impression of you, and it may affect how they introduce themselves. Consider learning in advance about your region's traditional Native introduction practices. These may refer to clans or ancestry, for example, "My name is June La Marr. My father's name was _____ and my mother's name was _____."

Explain to participants:

As facilitators, we will be doing some talking, but we would like to hear from you. We have something to offer to you, but we also know that you have wisdom to offer the group, too. So please feel free to share some of your wisdom. We are interested in your feedback and suggestions.

Now before we get started, we need to think about how we as a group can make the best use of this time. So we need to set up a few rules that might make the sessions run more smoothly.

One of the rules might be: Any personal information shared in the group will be kept confidential. For instance, I might share something personal so I would like you to keep that information to yourselves.

Duplicating this page is illegal. Do not copy without publisher's written permission.

17

Write "Confidentiality" on the poster board.

Ask:

Can you think of any other rules?

Generate a list of rules from participants and write them on the board. Ask other participants for feedback on suggested rules and refine them together as needed.

> ▶ **Facilitator Tip**
> If participants are having difficulty coming up with rules, suggest some of those below. (The last rule is meant to be lighthearted and to help generate conversation.)

Possible rules might include:

- Respect each other during and after the session.
- Don't interrupt if someone else is speaking.
- Don't carry on a conversation with someone else when others are talking.
- Don't make fun of one another's responses.
- Don't throw things at the speaker when he or she is speaking. (Just kidding!)

After the participants have come up with a list of rules, explain in your own words:

All of these are good rules and they will help us to get the most out of the sessions.

The Circle and the Medicine Wheel

This discussion helps students realize the connection between the circle and the Medicine Wheel. This is accomplished by showing how the Medicine Wheel is created using the circle— a Native American symbol.

Explain to participants:

We are going to be using the circle as a way to teach the life skills that will be presented in these sessions. The circle is very symbolic for Native people.

It represents a variety of concepts:

- **It signifies wholeness and our connection to the whole world.**
- **It is a powerful symbol of harmony and wellness.**
- **It signifies the never-ending cycle of life.**
- **It symbolizes the individual journey that each of us must take to find our way in life.**
- **It shows that making progress or growth is circular or cyclical in nature. The entire universe moves and works in circles.**

Many tribes have different names for the circle: Medicine Wheel, Sacred Hoop, Sacred Circle, Wheel of Life, and Circle of Life.

Ask:

Can you think of circular shapes in nature?

Write the responses on the board. Possible answers might include:

- the sun
- the moon
- the earth

Explain in your own words:

The circular shape represents the earth, the sun, the moon, the cycles of life, the seasons, and day to night. The Medicine Wheel that I will be presenting is just one of many versions, but the emphasis for all sacred circles remains the same: harmony, balance, and the interconnectedness of all things.

Ask:

How many of you are familiar with the meaning of the Circle of Life, Sacred Hoops, Sacred Circles, or Medicine Wheels?

Allow for responses.

Ask:

What do they mean to you?

Allow some time for the participants to discuss these concepts.

Ask the following before distributing handout 1.1:

Could you describe to me what a Medicine Wheel is?

> ▶ **Facilitator Tip**
> If participants do not respond, continue with the Medicine Wheel handout.

HANDOUT 1.1

Give each participant a copy of handout 1.1, "Medicine Wheel Significance."

Explain in your own words:

The Medicine Wheel is viewed as the circle of life. It is often used to represent the four directions: North, South, East, and West; the four seasons: summer, fall, winter, and spring; and the four parts of self: physical, mental, emotional, and spiritual. The following story by Black Elk shows the significance of the Medicine Wheel.

> ▶ **Facilitator Tip**
> Storytelling is at the heart of Native American culture, and the stories in these sessions illustrate important points. Take time in advance to reflect on them and practice telling them. They may be read aloud, but preferably they are told by heart.

Explain:

Black Elk, an Oglala Lakota traditional healer and visionary, wrote about the circle's significance. His people called it the Sacred Hoop.

Tell the following story.

Black Elk's Story

"In the old days when we were a strong and happy people, all of our power came to us from the sacred hoop of the nation, and so long as the hoop was unbroken, the people flourished. The flowering tree was the living center of the hoop, and the circle of the four quarters nourished it. The East gave peace and light, the South gave warmth, the West gave rain, and the North with its cold and mighty winds gave us strength and

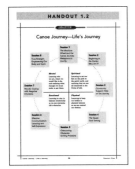

endurance. This knowledge came to us from the outer world with our religion.

"Everything the power of the world does is done in a circle. The sky is round like a ball, and I heard that the earth is round like a ball, and so are all stars. The wind in its greatest power, whirls. Birds make their nests in circles, for theirs is the same religion as ours. The sun comes forth and goes down again in a circle. The moon does the same and both are round. Even the seasons form a great circle in their changing, and always come back again to where they were. The life of a man is a circle from childhood to childhood and so it is in everything where power moves. Our tepees were round like the nests of birds, and these were set in a circle, the nation's hoop, a nest of many nests, where the Great Spirit means for us to hatch our children."

REPRINTED WITH PERMISSION.

Explain:

Black Elk's words teach us that the circle is a very important symbol of Native people. And the circle is used in countless ways to instruct us in Native American traditional teachings.

Preparing for Our Canoe Journey

This section provides an overview of a modern-day canoe journey. To ready ourselves for this journey, we need to strengthen our minds, emotions, spiritual beliefs, and our bodies. The canoe journey becomes a metaphor for the journey we take through life.

Give each participant a copy of handout 1.2, "Canoe Journey—Life's Journey."

HANDOUT 1.2

▶ **Facilitator Tip**
After distributing the handout, point out how the mental, spiritual, emotional, and physical aspects of the Medicine Wheel are linked to the eight session titles.

Explain in your own words:

The Canoe Image

Another image that we will use in teaching the life skills is the Northwest Native canoe journey. For hundreds of years the Natives in the Northwest were dependent on the traditional dugout canoe for fishing, whale hunting, travel, and all aspects of life. The oceangoing canoe was the very foundation of the Northwest Native culture. One elder said about the ocean, "I want the sea, that is my country." In other words, the ocean held great significance for him and his people.

The Resurgence of the Canoe

Around the turn of the twentieth century, gas engine boats began replacing canoes and all canoes except for the racing canoe disappeared.

The resurgence of the canoe journey began around the time of the "Paddle to Seattle" in 1989. A series of "paddles" occurred after that. Northwest tribes began returning to the great tradition of the dugout cedar canoes and soon many Native communities were inspired to build canoes and again become canoe nations.

The Modern Canoe Journey

A modern-day canoe journey is initiated for reasons other than survival. One elder wrote about the canoe journey, "We see the canoe journey as a vehicle for the discovery of ourselves and the ways of our ancestors."

So the purpose of the modern-day canoe journey is first, to honor the ancestors, and second, to learn traditional customs to promote self-discovery. It is also a metaphor that provides insight for the journey we take through life. Just as a canoe journey is difficult and arduous, so too is life's journey. Both journeys require courage, stamina, determination, and strength of spirit and character. They require using all the aspects of ourselves: our minds, our emotions, our spiritual beliefs, and our physical bodies to complete the journey.

Ask:

Are any of you familiar with what is involved in going on a canoe journey? If you're not, maybe you can visualize what it might be like. Use your imagination and picture it.

Allow time for participants to respond.

> ▶ **Facilitator Tip**
> If nobody is familiar with what occurs on a canoe journey, or doesn't respond, you can explain that the journey involves knowing numerous skills, and is guided by Native principles and beliefs.

HANDOUT 1.3

Give each participant a copy of handout 1.3, "Native American Beliefs."

Explain in your own words:

This handout on Native American beliefs will help you understand some background behind the significance of the Medicine Wheel. Throughout these sessions, we'll refer to these beliefs as applied to the skills we're learning.

Have the participants take turns reading each of the ten Native American Beliefs.

Ask:

What do you think is needed for a successful canoe journey?

Write the responses on the board. Possible answers might include:
- a sturdy canoe
- people who are strong, fit, and flexible
- good communication with others in the canoe
- teamwork to paddle and pull together
- clear goals and a way to achieve those goals
- knowing where you are going and how to get there
- commitment and the skills to maintain it
- knowledge to handle problems or emergencies that arise
- preparation
- a lot of support
- ability to follow directions
- ability to make wise decisions while in the canoe

After the participants have come up with a list, review the possible answers listed above and suggest any they might have missed.

Comparing the Canoe Journey to Life's Journey

In this section, students begin to see the correlation between the Canoe Journey and life's journey. The Elder's Story helps to show the spiritual nature of such a canoe journey and the importance of community. It also prepares the participants for determining what skills they'll need to bring along.

> ▶ **Facilitator Tip**
> As noted earlier, stories are best told by heart, but may be read aloud.

Tell the Elder's Story.

Elder's Story

An elder from the Tulalip Tribes named Della Hill was gracious enough to share some information about the canoe journey that her family and tribe participate in. The Tulalip Tribes Reservation is located in Washington, and is about forty miles north of Seattle.

Della said that every year the canoe families from many coastal communities join in a canoe journey together. The journeys take several weeks to complete, and there are usually many canoes on these journeys. As they travel and visit different communities, other canoes will join them along the way. One community is designated as the host community and the journey ends in that community. According to Della, the canoe journey is a spiritual journey.

She said that the pullers usually spend six to eight hours a day in the canoe. The canoes typically have two crews that paddle in three- to four-hour shifts.

Helpers on the Journey

There are many people who participate in the journey besides the people who are actually in the canoe. The others are helpers who travel by land to the different sites to set up camp for the pullers after they reach their destination for the day. The helpers dismantle the camp every morning while the pullers go on their way.

Della said that each day begins with a prayer and breakfast. Then before they embark on the day's journey, the group typically joins hands in a circle, asking the Creator to guide and care for them on the journey.

Each canoe has special songs that are sung throughout the journey.

On the journey, the pullers stop at several tribal communities that are on the way to their final destination. The tribal communities know that the pullers are coming and wait on shore to welcome them to the community.

Each canoe is individually greeted into the community with a prayer and a song as an invitation to the community.

Life Is a Journey

Ask:

So why are we talking about canoe journeys?

Allow for responses.

Explain in your own words:

We are comparing the canoe journey to life's journey for several reasons. I mentioned the courage and stamina that it takes, but can you think of other ways that a canoe journey is comparable to life's journey?

Allow for responses from participants and write them down so the class can view them.

Duplicating this page is illegal. Do not copy without publisher's written permission.

25

Explain further:

The point is that you live life without a plan, without preparation, without the skills to get through, without meaningful goals, without a good plan for taking care of yourself. But where does that get you?

Ask:

What does *not* having a good plan for life's journey lead to?

Allow for responses from participants and write them down so the class can view them.

Explain in your own words:

It can lead to depression, drug and alcohol abuse, anxiety, poor physical health, being stressed out, and for many people, suicide.

So by comparing our journey through life with a canoe journey, we can benefit from knowing what is needed to complete an actual traditional canoe journey.

So how can we make our lives like a well-planned journey?

Allow for responses from participants and write them down so the class can view them.

Explain in your own words:

One small way is by learning what is taught in these sessions. We can think of the skills that we learn as tools or paddles that we can use to complete our journey, just as the pullers use many paddles to complete their journey.

Give each participant a copy of handout 1.4, "Skills for Life's Journey."

Explain in your own words:

As with learning to handle a canoe, skills in all areas of our lives must be learned and practiced.

HANDOUT 1.4

Obstacles on the Journey

This discussion shows that no matter how much planning you do for a journey, obstacles arise. Specific obstacles focused on here are alcohol and drugs. Once again, storytelling helps the participant envision specific obstacles that might arise for them.

Explain and ask:

In our journey through life there are many obstacles that hinder us from progressing. Can you think of any obstacles that you might have on a canoe journey?

Write the responses on the board. Possible answers might include:

- Someone on the canoe is not willing to do his part
- We have bad weather
- The canoe develops a leak
- Everyone wants to quit

> ▶ **Facilitator Tip**
> Remember, stories are best told by heart, but may be read aloud.

Tell the Whale Story.

Whale Story

The Tulalip elder mentioned an obstacle that her group encountered one year while on a canoe journey. She said that on one canoe journey, the canoes came upon a strait and were having difficulty getting through it. Straits are difficult because you have two bodies of water converging and this tends to create a whirlpool effect.

Several of the canoes tried to get through the strait, but were unsuccessful. They paddled as hard as they could but made very little progress. While contemplating this obstacle, the pullers noticed a pod of Orcas swimming nearby. The Tulalip group decided that they had to try to get through the strait because they couldn't just sit there. So they went for it! They started paddling as hard as they could, but seemed to be getting nowhere. Just when they started to think about

Duplicating this page is illegal. Do not copy without publisher's written permission.

27

giving up, the Orcas that were nearby proceeded to pass by their canoe, one on each side, one pair at a time. This had the effect of moving the canoe forward. The canoe started to move. The pullers kept on paddling and found they were progressing through the strait. They were very thankful to the Orcas because they knew that they could not have passed through this obstacle without the help of the whales.

The pullers were amazed at what happened! As they watched the whales leave, the very last Orca dived in the water, and as he slipped below the surface his tail fin came out of the water and started flapping. The pullers knew that it meant that the Orcas were saying goodbye to them.

Comment:

Isn't that a wonderful story! Sometimes we have obstacles that seem insurmountable and we need divine intervention. It appears that those pullers received that kind of intervention.

Use of Drugs and Alcohol

Explain in your own words:

One obstacle that appears to be a problem for many young people today is the use of alcohol and drugs. We will be addressing issues related to drug and alcohol use throughout these sessions.

There are eight sessions in this curriculum. In addition to the session's topic, we will also discuss:

- **Native traditional beliefs that are associated with living a balanced, meaningful, and happy life**
- **various drugs and the risks associated with using them**
- **what we have learned in each session using the Medicine Wheel**

Before we look at some facts on alcohol, I'd like to give you some true-or-false questions about alcohol. First, fill out this questionnaire yourselves, then we'll review it as a group.

HANDOUT 1.5

Give each participant a copy of handout 1.5, "What Do You Know About Alcohol Use?" and let them fill it out themselves. Then read the questions aloud one by one, discuss the correct answers, and identify who had the most correct.

Correct answers are shown below.

1. True   5. True   8. True

2. False   6. True   9. False

3. False   7. True   10. True

4. True

> ▶ **Facilitator tip**
> If appropriate, have participants brainstorm about the answer to question 2. What should they do if a friend drinks too much and passes out? Offer guidance: they could get medical help, call 911, involve family members, and so on.

Explain in your own words:

Before we look at the next handout, let's consider what we know about how long-term alcohol use affects the body.

Ask and allow time for answers:

If you use alcohol for an extended period of time, what are some of the ways that it will affect your body?

Possible answers might include:

- alcohol can kill you

- if you drink too much, you can become an alcoholic

- it can affect your liver

- you can gain weight

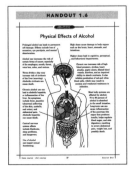

HANDOUT 1.6

Distribute handout 1.6, "Physical Effects of Alcohol," and discuss its contents.

Ask and allow time for answers:

- **Do you know what alcohol dependence is?**

- **How do you know if a friend has a problem with drinking?**

HANDOUT 1.7

• **How do you know if a friend has consumed too much alcohol?**

• **Do you know the dangers of overdose?**

Say:

The next handout will give us some answers.

Distribute handout 1.7, "Alcohol Use/Abuse," and review the contents to cover the answers to the above questions.

Then ask:

Would you want to take alcohol on a canoe journey?

Allow for responses.

Explain and ask:

So that leads to the question that each of us should ask ourselves: "Do I want alcohol to be a part of my life's journey?"

TRADITIONAL NATIVE BELIEF

Explain this traditional Native belief:

In order to experience true learning, each of the four dimensions of the Medicine Wheel—the physical, the mental, the emotional, and the spiritual—must be addressed.

Conclusion

Here we summarize what has been learned throughout this session using the Medicine Wheel.

Give each participant a copy of handout 1.8, "What Did You Learn?"

Draw a Medicine Wheel on the board.

HANDOUT 1.8

▶ **Facilitator Tip**
Draw the Medicine Wheel as shown on the handout. Make two intersecting arrows, vertical and horizontal, creating four quandrants: mental (upper left); spiritual (upper right); physical (lower right); and emotional (lower left). If you have a small group, you can simply show a copy of the handout to illustrate your point and write on that.

30

Ask:

Using the Medicine Wheel's four dimensions, what could we say we have learned in this session?

Allow for responses. Possible answers might include:

Mental

- traditional Native beliefs
- Sacred Circles, in particular the Medicine Wheel
- how to complete a Canoe Journey successfully
- what makes us healthy mentally

Spiritual

- the spiritual nature of the canoe journey itself
- the spiritual nature of the Medicine Wheel

Physical

- physical stamina, strength, and energy required for a canoe journey
- the fact that life's journey is also arduous
- what makes us healthy physically

Emotional

- emotional balance required for a canoe journey
- the full range of emotions required to complete the journey successfully

As participants give answers, ask questions to prompt discussion. You might ask, "Can anyone think of an example from their own life?" After the discussion, have students fill out the handout.

> ▶ **Facilitator Tip**
> Participants should be given time to complete the handouts while in the session. Do not allow the participants to take the assignments home.

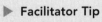

Duplicating this page is illegal. Do not copy without publisher's written permission.

31

Medicine Wheel Significance

North
Color: White
Meaning: Purity, wisdom, and healing cures
Stage of Life: Elder
Season: Winter
Sacred Plant: With sweet grass we pray for protection from evil and for safe travel.

West
Color: Black
Meaning: Reflection and spiritual insight
Stage of Life: Adulthood
Season: Autumn
Sacred Plant: With sage we pray for purification of the body and good health.

Mental *Spiritual*

Emotional *Physical*

East
Color: Yellow
Meaning: Potential for learning; respect for the dignity of everything around us
Stage of life: Childhood
Season: Spring
Sacred plant: With tobacco we pray to the spirit world, asking for renewal of life.

South
Color: Red
Meaning: Knowledge; harmony with our environment and with others; full-blooming abundance
Stage of Life: Adolescence
Season: Summer
Sacred Plant: With cedar we pray for purification of the body and protection from evil.

Canoe Journey—Life's Journey

Session 1

The Medicine Wheel and the Canoe Journey: Metaphors to Live By

Session 8

True Strength: Empowering Our Body and Spirit

Session 2

Beginning at the Center: Who Am I?

Mental

Learning who we are, where we would like to be, and realizing what changes we must make to get there.

Spiritual

Learning to set our feet on the path to the spirit world, and realizing that we are all connected in the Circle of Life.

Session 7

Moods: Coping with Negative Emotions

Session 3

Community Support: Help on the Journey

Emotional

Learning to stay in balance emotionally so we can overcome life's obstacles.

Physical

Learning to keep our bodies in physical balance so we can control our destiny.

Session 6

Effective Communication: Listening and Self-Expression

Session 4

The Quest: Goal Setting

Session 5

Overcoming Obstacles: Solving Problems

Native American Beliefs

- There are powerful unseen forces or powers that play important roles in our lives. These powers may take the form of deities or they may be more of a "feeling" that something exists and is sacred and mysterious.

- The seen and the unseen are equally important. The physical world is real, the spiritual world is real; they are two aspects of one reality. Yet there are separate laws that govern each of them. A balanced life is one that honors both.

- All things are interrelated and all things have life (spiritual energy). Everything is part of a whole and each element in the universe has its place and its function. Hence, all things are worthy of respect and reverence. The sacred relationship we have with the universe is to be honored.

- In order to be well, people must abide by beliefs about the balance between man and nature and the importance of maintaining balance and harmony in our lives.

- Everyone and everything was created with a specific purpose to fulfill. No one should have the power to interfere or to impose on others the best path to follow. What is required is that we seek our place in the universe and everything else will follow in good time.

- Human beings have the ability to learn new skills, but they must be willing to do so through life lessons and elder teachings.

- Change is constant but occurs in cycles or patterns. Change is not accidental or random. Human beings must be active participants in the changes in their lives.

- All desire to change comes from within and the doorway to change is having the volition (or will) to change. The right path will always be there. What must be determined is what happens to bring a person to a point where they will decide to follow the path.

- The spiritual dimension of human development consists of four areas: visions, spiritual teachings, ideals, and dreams and goals. Having the experience of any of these symbolizes a need for change and they serve as a guide for future action.

- Elders are honored and respected because of the lifetime's worth of wisdom they have acquired. The family is based on a multigenerational support system of interdependence that provides cultural continuity for all. The tribe is an interdependent system of people who perceive themselves as parts of the greater whole.

Source: Bopp, J., Bopp, M., Brown, L., and Lane, P. (1989). *The Sacred Tree,* 3rd edition. Lethbridge, Alberta, Canada: Four Worlds Development Press. Used with permission.

Skills for Life's Journey

Learning from the Medicine Wheel

Learning from the canoe journey

Self-awareness/Spiritual well-being

Connection to community

Setting goals

Problem solving/Decision making

Communication

Effective listening

Assertiveness

Coping with emotions

Anger management

Conflict resolution

Stress reduction

Making decisions about alcohol and drug use

Maintaining good health

Preparing for the future

What Do You Know About Alcohol Use?

Next to each statement, circle "**T**" for true or "**F**" for false.

❶ Three drinks a day may increase risk for cirrhosis of the liver.   T   F

❷ If a friend drinks too much alcohol and passes out, it's best to just let them sleep it off.   T   F

❸ Prolonged use of alcohol cannot cause permanent damage to brain cells.   T   F

❹ Having one drink in the morning could mean you have a problem with alcohol.   T   F

❺ Most body systems are affected by alcohol.   T   F

❻ Drinking alcohol can put you at risk for developing some types of cancer.   T   F

❼ Chronic use of alcohol can cause heart attacks.   T   F

❽ Feeling bad or guilty about your drinking may be an indication that you have a drinking problem.   T   F

❾ Having a high tolerance to alcohol means you get drunk faster.   T   F

❿ Alcoholism and alcohol dependence are the same thing.   T   F

Physical Effects of Alcohol

Prolonged alcohol use leads to permanent cell damage. Effects include loss of sensation, eye paralysis, and mental deterioration.

Alcohol use increases the risk of certain forms of cancer, especially of the esophagus, mouth, throat, voice box, colon, and rectum.

Three drinks a day may increase risk of cirrhosis of the liver (scarring). Alcoholic cirrhosis can cause death.

Chronic alcohol use can lead to alcoholic hepatitis, or inflammation of the liver. Its symptoms include fever, jaundice (abnormal yellowing of the skin, eyeballs, and urine), and abdominal pain. Alcoholic hepatitis can cause death.

Central nervous system effects include blackouts, sleep problems, and hangovers.

Use of alcohol can impair sexual functioning.

High doses cause damage to body organs such as the brain, heart, stomach, and intestines.

Higher doses lead to cognitive, perceptual, and behavioral impairments.

Chronic use increases risk of high blood pressure, strokes, heart attacks, peptic ulcers, dilated blood vessels, diarrhea, and an impaired ability to absorb nutrients. It also inhibits production of red and white blood cells, which may result in anemia and weakened resistance to infection.

Most body systems are affected by alcohol; 70 to 80 percent of alcohol is absorbed in the small intestine. Long-term use can cause inflammation of the pancreas (the organ that produces insulin, helps regulate blood sugar, and aids digestion), resulting in severe abdominal pain, weight loss, and possibly death.

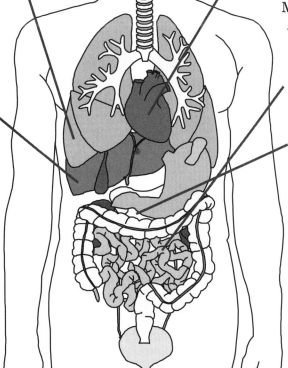

Alcohol Use/Abuse

Alcoholism, also known as alcohol dependence, is a disease that includes these four symptoms:

1. Craving: a strong need or urge to drink

2. Loss of control: inability to stop drinking

3. Physical dependence: the body depends on alcohol, and quitting can lead to withdrawal symptoms such as nausea, sweating, shakiness, and anxiety

4. Tolerance: the need to drink greater amounts of alcohol to get high

What is important to know?

About half an ounce of alcohol equals a standard drink. This equates to:
- one shot of distilled spirits (80 proof), or
- one 5-ounce glass of wine, or
- one 12-ounce beer

It is illegal to buy or possess alcohol if you are under age 21.

What is blood alcohol concentration (BAC)?

The amount of alcohol in a person's body is measured by its weight in a certain volume of blood: the blood alcohol concentration, or BAC. (Alcohol is absorbed directly through the walls of the stomach and the small intestine, enters the bloodstream, and travels throughout the body and to the brain.) Most states in the United States have passed a law making it illegal to drive with a BAC of .08 or higher.

How do I know if a friend has a problem with drinking?

Your friend's responses to these four questions may give you the answer.
- Have you ever felt you should cut down on your drinking?
- Have people annoyed you by criticizing your drinking?
- Have you ever felt bad or guilty about your drinking?
- Have you ever had a drink first thing in the morning to steady your nerves or to get rid of a hangover?

One "yes" suggests a possible alcohol problem. More than one "yes" means a problem is highly likely. A medical doctor or health care provider should be consulted to determine if there is an alcohol problem and recommend the best course of action.

CONTINUED ON NEXT PAGE

Alcohol's General Effects and Effects on Driving

BAC BLOOD ALCOHOL CONCENTRATION	TYPICAL EFFECTS	PREDICTABLE EFFECTS ON DRIVING
.02%	• some loss of judgment • relaxation • slight body warmth • altered mood	• decline in visual functions (such as ability to track a rapidly moving target) • trouble doing two tasks at one time (dividing attention)
.05%	• exaggerated behavior • possible loss of small-muscle control (such as focusing eyes) • impaired judgment	• reduced coordination • reduced ability to track moving objects • difficulty steering • slower response to emergency situations
.08%	• poor muscle coordination (balance, speech, vision, reaction time, hearing) • trouble detecting danger • impaired judgment, self-control, reasoning, memory	• poor concentration • short-term memory loss • poor speed control • poor information processing (such as signal detection, visual searching) • impaired perception
.10%	• clear deterioration of reaction time and control • slurred speech, poor coordination, slowed thinking	• reduced ability to maintain lane position and brake appropriately
.15%	• far less muscle control than normal • possible vomiting (unless BAC level is reached slowly or drinker has a tolerance for alcohol) • major loss of balance	• substantial impairment in vehicle control, attention to driving task, and ability to process information, through both eyes and ears

Source: Adapted from chart "The ABCs of BAC," retrieved Jan. 19, 2007 from http://stopimpaireddriving.org/ABCsBACWeb/page2.htm

What are the danger signs of overdose?

Alcohol poisoning is a potentially fatal physical reaction to an alcohol overdose or binge drinking. Symptoms of alcohol poisoning include:

- vomiting
- unconsciousness
- cold, clammy, pale, or bluish skin; and/or
- slow or irregular breathing (less than 8 breaths a minute, or 10 or more seconds between breaths)

When excessive alcohol is consumed, the brain is deprived of oxygen. After struggling to deal with the overdose, the brain eventually shuts down the involuntary functions that regulate breathing and heart rate. At a BAC of .35, consciousness is at the level of surgical anesthesia. At .60, chances are the drinker will be dead.

Source: National Institute on Alcohol Abuse and Alcoholism, www.niaaa.nih.gov.

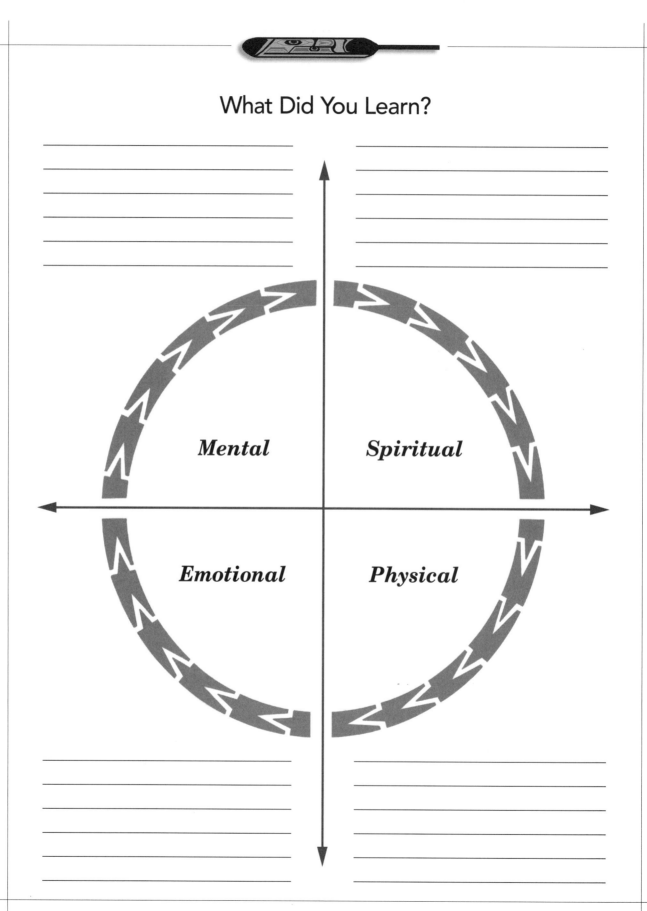

What Did You Learn?

Mental

Spiritual

Emotional

Physical

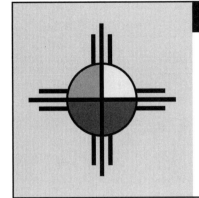

Who Am I?

BEGINNING AT THE CENTER

Purpose of Session 2

This session teaches adolescents about themselves, their values, and their character strengths. It also shows how marijuana use can conflict with one's established values and integrity.

Learner Outcomes

By the end of this session, participants will be able to:

- use the Medicine Wheel as a way to define themselves

- interpret the term "self-awareness"

- discover what their values are

- explain what "integrity" is, and name their character strengths

- explain how using marijuana can conflict with their integrity and values

Materials Needed

- ☐ flip chart, white board, or chalk board
- ☐ markers or chalk
- ☐ handout 2.1, *Who Am I?*
- ☐ handout 2.2, *What Is Important to Me? What Are My Values?*
- ☐ handout 2.3, *My Character Strengths*
- ☐ handout 2.4, *What Do You Know about Marijuana Use?*
- ☐ handout 2.5, *Marijuana*
- ☐ handout 2.6, *What Did You Learn?*

Preparation Needed

1. Read session 2 in its entirety to become familiar with it.

2. If you've provided binders or folders for participants, bring them along and distribute them at the start of the session.

3. Photocopy all handouts and hole-punch if needed. Handouts appear in this book after each session outline; they can also be printed from the CD-ROM (if using a color printer, decorative elements will appear in color). During the session, distribute them one by one as prompted.

4. Arrange the room so that each participant can be included in the conversation.

5. If you created ground rules in session 1, post them for all participants to view.

6. For the "Who Am I?" portion of this session, be ready to draw three pie charts: the two charts shown on page 45, and one depicting your own balance of "self" elements.

Who Am I?

This session might be compared to preparing for a trip. But this activity doesn't just focus on physical items: it considers the whole self. Here, participants will be provided a chance to explore the spiritual, physical, mental, and emotional sides of themselves. They also draw pie charts that show how they perceive themselves.

Ask:

When undertaking a canoe journey, what do we need to know about ourselves?

Allow for answers.

Ask:

Why is it important to know about ourselves before we start the journey?

Allow for answers.

Explain to participants:

We learned in session 1 about the Medicine Wheel and how the four directions represent the spiritual, mental, physical, and emotional sides of many things, including ourselves.

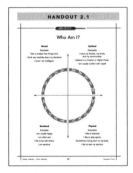

HANDOUT 2.1

Give each participant a copy of handout 2.1, "Who Am I?"

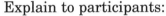

Defining Ourselves

Explain in your own words:

We'd like you to identify different aspects of yourself and write them down in the different sections of your handout. To get you started, let's start with the spiritual side.

Ask:

What is the spiritual side of you like? What do you value?

Possible answers might include:

- Being aware of anything that is unseen
- Believing in God or a Higher Power
- Thinking that we have a purpose in life
- Honoring our inner values

Duplicating this page is illegal. Do not copy without publisher's written permission.

43

Ask:

What is the physical side of you like?

Possible answers might include:

- I like to be physically fit
- I like to feed my body healthy food
- I like to do things that are relaxing
- I hate exercise

Ask:

What is the emotional side of you like?

- I am a sensitive person
- I am sometimes moody
- I am sometimes happy
- I am a loving and caring person

Ask:

What is the mental side of you like?

- I think about who I am
- I think positive thoughts and negative thoughts
- I think about my future
- I think about doing things that are not good for me

After prompting these examples, give participants time to write down their own answers on the handout. Encourage them to look at the other examples on the handout to help get them started.

Explain in your own words:

While most of us have physical, emotional, spiritual, and mental aspects, we don't necessarily have them in equal measure. It depends on who we are.

Draw the following diagrams on the board or on a flip chart so participants can view it easily. Make a circle and divide it into four unequal parts, representing a person with a particular mix of the mental, spiritual, physical, and emotional aspects.

Ask the question:

What kind of person does this diagram represent?

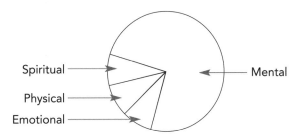

Have participants guess.

Explain in your own words:

This is a person who is mostly focused on the mental aspect of himself or herself, and maybe is the kind of person who works as a computer programmer or an engineer.

Ask:

And what kind of person does this diagram represent?

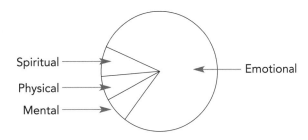

Have participants guess.

Explain in your own words:

This is a person who is mostly focused on emotions and maybe is the kind of person who works as an artist or an actor.

Now I would like each of you to draw a diagram that best describes what you are like. I will do it first.

Draw a pie chart that represents your own personality. Then ask each participant to do the same, taking turns at the board or flip chart.

Explain in your own words:

From this exercise we have learned more about you. But more than that, we have learned how you perceive yourself.

What Are My Values?

In this section, participants ask themselves what they value. They begin by identifying someone who is their role model. On the handout "What Is Important to Me? What Are My Values?" they write down some of the things they value most. Then they compare their values with their mentors' values.

Explain in your own words:

Now we are going to talk about what is important to you. In other words, what your *values* are. I would like you to think of a person you really admire. What are the things that you admire about the person?

> ▶ **Facilitator Tip**
> As shown here, you might want to provide the example of Martin Luther King, Jr. and ask students to describe some of his character traits.

Explain:

A possible example might be Martin Luther King, Jr.

Ask:

What are some examples of King's character traits?

Allow for responses, and prompt these if needed.

- He stood up for what is right
- He was a good leader
- He was a religious person
- He was a courageous person
- He was a nonviolent person

Now ask:

Now I'd like each of you to name another person and identify what you admire about that person. It can be a person you know, or a person in the public eye.

Allow time for each participant to identify a person and list some attributes.

Ask each participant:

Does this person have qualities that you would like to have yourself? And why is that?

HANDOUT 2.2

Explain in your own words:

Typically, we admire someone because they have values that we appreciate. So basically, the good (or bad) values we see in others are values that are important to us.

Give each participant a copy of handout 2.2, "What Is Important to Me? What Are My Values?"

Explain:

Write down your values on the handout.

Allow time to complete.

Ask:

Do any of your values match with your mentor's? If so, which ones?

Allow for discussion and then move on to the next topic, integrity.

Integrity and Character Strengths

In this section, participants see the value of integrity. They'll be provided an opportunity to discover what someone who has integrity is like. They will discover that people with integrity are not only honest with others, but more importantly, honest with themselves.

Duplicating this page is illegal. Do not copy without publisher's written permission.

47

INTEGRITY

Explain in your own words:

Now we are going to talk about how we live by our values.

Ask:

Does anyone know what "integrity" is?

Allow participants to respond.

Explain in your own words:

A person who has integrity is usually someone who has values and adheres to those values. They are usually honest with others, but most of all, they are honest with themselves.

Draw this diagram on the board or on a flip chart and refer to it when giving the example.

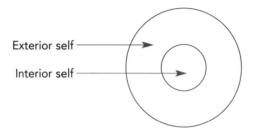

Explain in your own words:

Values are part of our inner or interior self. If we show those values on the outside or exterior, we are demonstrating integrity.

Do you know people who sometimes are not the same on the outside as they are on the inside?

Allow for responses.

Explain in your own words:

We usually call these people fakes or phonies. Here is an example of one of these kinds of people. Let's say that you are someone who has values about being truthful and honest. Your friend asks you to go to the store with her and shoplift.

If you say no and explain that you don't want to steal, how will taking that stand make you feel?

Allow for responses.

But if you give in and go with your friend and shoplift, how will you feel?

Allow for responses.

Ask:

Do you see how important it is to adhere to our values?

Explain in your own words:

If we do not adhere to our inner values, we will lose our self-respect and eventually it will erode any positive self-esteem that we have.

Ask:

Why do you think having positive self-esteem will help you on your life journey?

Allow for responses.

HANDOUT 2.3

CHARACTER STRENGTHS

Give each participant a copy of handout 2.3, "My Character Strengths."

Explain in your own words:

This handout on character strengths will further help you determine what is important to you. Think about where you fall on the spectrum between the two opposites shown, and place a dot there.

Give participants time to complete the survey.

Explain in your own words:

Sometimes it's useful to complete an assignment like this to help you learn more about yourself.

Ask:

Does the outside world see the character strengths that you've identified here?

Allow for responses.

Marijuana

In this discussion students see how one drug, marijuana, can impact their values and integrity. The larger question is then posed: "Is this something we want to take along on a canoe or life journey?" Be prepared for lively conversation.

Explain in your own words:

Drugs can conflict with our values, integrity, and character strengths. For example, let's look at marijuana. How much do you already know about marijuana? Let's start by filling out this true-or-false questionnaire.

Give each participant a copy of handout 2.4, "What Do You Know About Marijuana Use?" Allow a few minutes for them to fill it out.

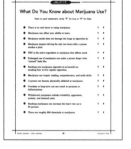

HANDOUT 2.4

Then say:

Now let's review the facts on this next handout and find the answers.

Pass out copies of handout 2.5, "Marijuana."

HANDOUT 2.5

Review the handout aloud with the group and find the answers to the true-or-false questionnaire.

Correct answers are shown below.

1. False	6. True	11. True
2. True	7. True	12. True
3. False	8. True	13. False
4. False	9. True	
5. True	10. True	

Ask:

Would we want to take marijuana on a canoe journey?

Allow for responses.

Explain:

So that leads to the question that each of us should ask ourselves, "Do I want marijuana to be a part of my life's journey?"

Allow for responses.

Explain:

One traditional Native belief that applies to this session says:

TRADITIONAL

NATIVE BELIEF

"All desire to change comes from within and the doorway to change is having the volition (or will) to change. The right path will always be there. What must be determined is what happens to bring a person to a point where they will decide to follow the path."

Ask:

In what way does this session relate to this belief?

Allow for responses.

Conclusion

HANDOUT 2.6

Here we summarize what has been learned throughout this session using the Medicine Wheel.

Give each participant a copy of handout 2.6, "What Did You Learn?"

Ask:

Using the Medicine Wheel's four dimensions, what could we say that we have learned in this session?

Give participants time to write on the handout answers in each of the four categories: mental, spiritual, physical, and emotional. You may choose to draw the Medicine Wheel on the board.

Under the appropriate categories, suggested responses might include:

Mental
- I have learned what my values are
- I now know what "integrity" means and how it pertains to me

Spiritual
- What I value in others
- What values are important to me
- How a lack of integrity affects me spiritually

Physical
- How my physical presence matches what I am on the inside
- How physical appearance plays out in my life

Emotional
- The importance of the emotional aspect
- How a lack of integrity affects my emotional side

Ask each participant to share an item or two from the handout. Ask questions to spark discussion.

> ▶ **Facilitator Tip**
> Participants should be given time to complete the handout during the session. Do not allow participants to take the assignments home.

Who Am I?

Mental

Examples:

I like to analyze how things work.

I think very carefully about my decisions.

I know I am intelligent.

Spiritual

Examples:

I value my friends, my family,
and my communities.

I believe in a Creator or Higher Power.

I am usually truthful with myself.

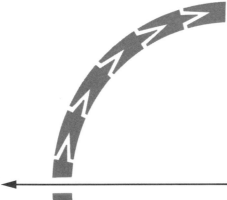

Emotional

Examples:

I am usually happy.

I am often sad.

I like to be with others.

I am sensitive.

Physical

Examples:

I like to exercise.

I like to play sports.

Sometimes I bring harm to my body.

I like to test my stamina.

What Is Important to Me? What Are My Values?

_____

_____

_____

_____

_____

_____

_____

_____

_____

_____

_____

_____

_____

_____

_____

_____

_____

_____

_____

_____

_____

_____

_____

My Character Strengths

Between these opposite characteristics is a line, making a spectrum.
Choose where you fit on that spectrum and make a dot there.

I am athletic. ⟷	I am not athletic.
I depend on others. ⟷	I don't depend on others.
I show feelings. ⟷	I don't show feelings.
I go along with others. ⟷	I do my own thing.
I get excited easily. ⟷	I am calm.
I take part in activities. ⟷	I prefer to be alone.
I want to win when I compete with others. ⟷	I don't care if I win.
I make sense. ⟷	Sometimes I don't make sense.
I keep things to myself. ⟷	I am open with others.

What Do You Know about Marijuana Use?

Next to each statement, circle "**T**" for true or "**F**" for false.

❶ There is no real harm in using marijuana. T F

❷ Marijuana can affect your ability to learn. T F

❸ Marijuana smoke does not damage the lungs as cigarettes do. T F

❹ Marijuana impairs driving for only two hours after a person smokes a joint. T F

❺ THC is the active ingredient in marijuana that affects mood. T F

❻ Prolonged use of marijuana can make a person forget what "normal" feels like. T F

❼ Smoking one marijuana cigarette is as harmful as smoking four to five regular cigarettes. T F

❽ Marijuana can impair reading, comprehension, and math skills. T F

❾ A person can become physically addicted to marijuana. T F

❿ Overdose or long-term use can result in paranoia or hallucinations. T F

⓫ Withdrawal symptoms include irritability, aggression, anxiety, and stomach pain. T F

⓬ Smoking marijuana can increase the heart rate up to 50 percent. T F

⓭ There are roughly 800 chemicals in marijuana. T F

Marijuana

What is marijuana?

Marijuana is a mixture of dried, shredded flowers and leaves of the hemp plant *(Cannabis sativa)*. Of its 400 chemicals, THC (delta-9-tetrahydrocannabinol) has the strongest effect on the brain, altering mood, thinking, and behavior. An illegal drug, marijuana can be smoked or eaten in certain foods. Its effects vary depending on its THC content, the user's past experience with it, and how and where it is used (including presence of alcohol or other drugs).

Is it addictive? Yes. Research confirms that long-term use can lead to tolerance—the user needs more of it to get the same high—and to addiction. Withdrawal symptoms include irritability, aggression, anxiety, and stomach pain.

Slang terms: *Pot, weed, grass, boom, herb, Mary Jane, reefer.*

Common effects of initial use:

loss of coordination; slower reactions • relaxed feeling of well-being
rapid heartbeat (up to 50 percent faster) • confusion; short-term memory loss
bloodshot eyes; lower body temperature • increased appetite

Common effects of heavy use:

drowsiness and lack of concentration • further loss of coordination
trouble with problem solving, memory, and learning • depression or panic
distorted perception (sight, sound, touch, and passage of time)

Other adverse effects:

- Smoking one joint impairs driving for four to six hours.

- Marijuana impairs learning ability, including reading, comprehension, and math skills. In teens, it can stunt both short- and long-term development.

- Users often lack ambition and interest, have trouble concentrating and acting on long-term plans, and lose ground at school and work. A long-term user can forget what "normal" feels like.

- An overdose or long-term use can lead to hallucinations and paranoia.

- Marijuana can cause cancer. Like tobacco, it contains cancer-causing chemicals (one joint is as harmful as four to five tobacco cigarettes), it can cause coughing and wheezing, and it increases risk for pneumonia. It can also cause lung damage: users typically inhale and hold the smoke deeply to get the full effect.

What Did You Learn?

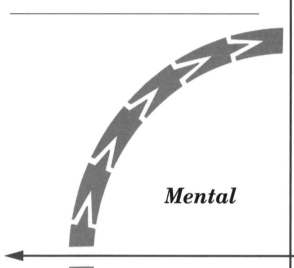

Mental *Spiritual*

Emotional *Physical*

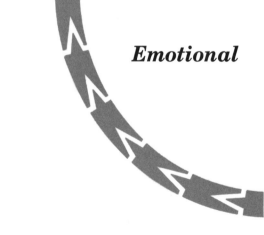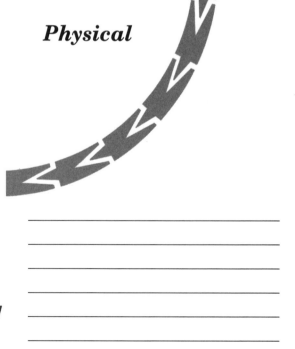

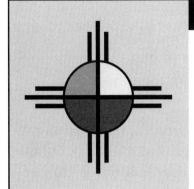

Community Support

HELP ON THE JOURNEY

Purpose of Session 3

In this session participants think about the communities they belong to. They learn about their role on this canoe journey as they look at the people around them. They will discuss how taking drugs such as club drugs or stimulants can disrupt a canoe journey.

Learner Outcomes

By the end of this session, participants will be able to:

• identify the importance of community

• describe how they are a part of many communities

• identify what a mentor is

• describe how to become a mentor

Materials Needed

☐ flip chart, white board, or chalk board

☐ markers or chalk

☐ handout 3.1, *The Communities Around You*

☐ handout 3.2, *Mentoring*

☐ handout 3.3, *Club Drugs*

☐ handout 3.4, *Stimulants*

☐ handout 3.5, *Club Drugs Worksheet* (one copy only)

☐ handout 3.6, *Stimulants Worksheet* (one copy only)

☐ handout 3.7, *What Did You Learn?*

Preparation Needed

1. Read session 3 in its entirety to become familiar with it.

2. If you've provided binders or folders for participants, bring them along to distribute at the start of the session.

3. Photocopy all handouts and hole-punch if needed. Handouts appear in this book after each session outline; they can also be printed from the CD-ROM (if using a color printer, decorative elements will appear in color). During the session, distribute them one by one as prompted.

4. Arrange the room so that each participant can be included in the conversation.

5. If you created ground rules in session 1, post them for all participants to view.

Support for the Journey

Explain in your own words:

So far we have talked about the canoe journey and the role you play if you are on the journey. Now we're going to talk about the other people who are in the canoe with you, pulling along with you and helping you out on your way.

Ask:

Why is it important to think about who is in the canoe with us?

Generate responses and write them on the board or flip chart.

Possible responses might include:

- If you like the other people involved, you will have more fun on the journey.
- If you like them, you will look forward to each day.
- There will be problems if you don't like others on the trip.
- If you don't like them, you won't work well together.
- If you don't like them, you won't enjoy the journey.
- If you don't like them, you might get into an argument with them.

After the participants have come up with a list, review the possible answers listed above and suggest any they might have missed.

Ask:

Why are others important on a canoe journey?

Generate responses and write them on the board or flip chart. Possible responses might include:

- Others can help us.
- It takes a group effort to complete a long canoe journey.
- Others can be companions.
- Others can provide encouragement.
- Others may have skills that we don't have.
- Others may be able to guide the canoe.
- Others are needed in dangerous situations.

After the participants have come up with a list, review the possible answers listed above and suggest any they might have missed.

Explain in your own words:

In thinking about people you may want to have on your life journey, we are going to discuss:
- **Family and extended family**
- **Community**
- **Mentors**

Explain:

One traditional Native belief that applies to family says:

TRADITIONAL NATIVE BELIEF

"The family is based on a multigenerational support system of interdependence that provides cultural continuity for all. The tribe is an interdependent system of people who perceive themselves as parts of the greater whole."

This teaching shows just how connected people actually are.

Family Support

Explain in your own words:

The traditional Native teaching says that family is the primary source of support. In the past, family and extended family were so important that they were considered critical to survival. As you may know, Native families tend to extend beyond the nuclear family of parents and children. The extended family usually includes grandparents, aunts, uncles, cousins, and even friends not related by blood. Extended family members share the responsibility for the whole family. These large families provide social, financial, and emotional support. They also share in the care of the children and help in times of crisis.

I know a woman who only has one granddaughter. But because her five sisters have many grandchildren, she is considered and called "grandma" by all of her sister's grandchildren.

Tribal Support

Explain in your own words:

People in the tribal community work together closely for the good of the community. The tribal communities are thought to be a large family where everyone is considered a relative, to a greater or lesser degree. In urban settings, where many people are far from their homes, organizations like the Seattle Indian Health Board provide the community-like atmosphere where Natives from many different areas can come together and be a part of a community.

Canoe Families

Explain in your own words:

Many of the participants on canoe journeys are related to one another, but some of the travelers are from other families. Yet they call themselves "canoe families."

Ask:

Why do you think that they would call themselves "canoe families"?

Allow for responses.

Explain:

The point is that they work together as a loving and supportive family would.

Community Support

Explain:

We can think about who is with us on our life journey in terms of our "community." Community can mean a lot of things.

Ask:

Imagine the tasks involved in a canoe journey. Who would you include in the community of people? What roles would they play?

Generate a list of responses and write them on the board or flip chart. Possible responses might include:

- pullers
- helpers
- leaders
- guides

After the participants have come up with a list, review them and suggest any they might have missed.

Ask:

Why are all of these parts of the community important for the canoe journey?

Allow participants time to respond.

Communities Around You

HANDOUT 3.1

Ask:

Can you think of some different communities you are a part of?

Allow participants time to respond.

Give each participant a copy of handout 3.1, "The Communities Around You."

To help the participants get started on filling in their handouts, write the word "You" in the center of the board or on a flip chart. Ask for suggestions on different communities we belong to. Feel free to write some of the suggestions on the board or flip chart to generate some conversation.

> ▶ **Facilitator Note**
> It's okay if participants name different communities than those listed on the next page. Just proceed in the exercise using the communities they mention. Chances are most responses will correspond with the communities listed on the example.

Examples might include:

THE COMMUNITIES AROUND YOU

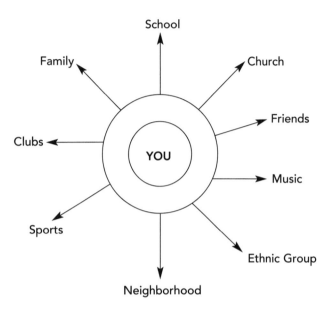

Community Skills

Explain in your own words:

In each of these communities, there are certain things you need to know in order to do well in that community—certain skills that help you get by. For example, at school you need to know how to get there on time, how to talk with your teachers, and lots of other things in order to do well.

Ask:

Can you think of other things you need to know or skills you need to have in order to do well in school?

Now go back to the chart you've just completed and write down responses next to the appropriate word (see below for an example regarding schools).

THE COMMUNITIES AROUND YOU

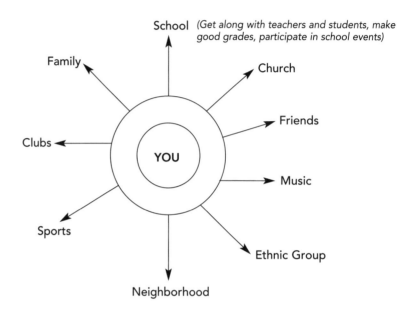

Ask:

What are things you need to know or skills you need to have in order to do well in other communities?

Write down participants' answers, and point out the similarities and differences.

Multiculturalism

Ask:

Have you ever noticed that in order to do well in a community, you have to know the language of that community? Have you noticed that the language for one community may not be the same for another community?

Explain in your own words:

For example, the language you use with your friends may be quite different from the language you use at home, at school, or in church. However, this does not mean that you are not honoring your integrity. It simply means that you are displaying skillful behavior in different social situations.

Explain in your own words:

Knowing how to do well in different communities is really important for our life journey because it gives us the chance to take something from each of these areas. Making the journey alone would be really hard. We need to know how we can draw something from each of these communities so that we can make the journey easier.

Mentoring

This discussion shows participants how a mentor can enhance both the canoe journey and life's journey. It also prepares them to become mentors themselves.

Explain in your own words:

Now let's go back to our canoe journey. We are going to get more specific and talk about the actual person paddling next to you, or in front of you, or behind you. When you think about who you want in the canoe with you, you might think of a lot of people. You might think of your friends because you have fun with them and trust them. We will also talk about older people you might want paddling with you or helping to guide your canoe.

Ask:

Who else might you like to have in the canoe with you besides your friends?

Allow the participants to respond.

Ask:

Is there any reason that you may want elders on the journey with you?

Allow the participants to respond.

Duplicating this page is illegal. Do not copy without publisher's written permission.

67

Ask:

Does anyone know what a mentor is?

Allow the participants to respond. Suggested responses may include:

- someone who cares
- someone you trust
- someone you respect
- someone who is an authority

Ask:

What are the things that a mentor could do for you?

Allow the participants to respond.

Ask:

In what ways are mentors similar to teachers and elders?

Allow for responses.

Explain:

There are some differences among teachers, elders, and mentors—but there are many more similarities.

TRADITIONAL
NATIVE BELIEF

Explain:

One traditional Native belief refers to the mentor role of elders:

"Elders are to be honored and respected because of the lifetime's worth of wisdom they have acquired."

Explain in your own words:

I know a woman who said that her father is her mentor because of all that he has accomplished. He came to this country without money and without a job. He eventually got a job. He worked very hard and made a good life for himself and his family.

Selecting a Mentor

Ask:

Who is or who could be a mentor to you?

Write responses on the board or flip chart. Make sure to raise the issue of trust and how an older person could be trustworthy and serve as a mentor. The list could include:

- a teacher or coach
- a counselor, pastor, or minister
- a friend's parent
- a relative
- an elder in the community

After the participants have come up with a list, review the possible answers listed above and suggest any they might have missed.

Mentor Attributes

Ask:

So what are attributes of a good mentor? How would you like your mentor to be?

List may include some of the following:

- has wisdom and is understanding
- is a good listener
- understands our beliefs
- possesses and uses faith
- is comfortable to be around
- is good-natured and happy
- possesses self-confidence
- is patient, honest, trustworthy, and caring
- has a loving, caring attitude

Explain in your own words:

We can see by this list that one mentor might not do everything for us. We can have various mentors who guide us in different areas of our lives. Just as there might be someone who is better at navigating the canoe, someone who is an expert in organizing the journey, or someone who is better

at guiding the crew through rough waters, we can have many mentors who mentor us in different areas.

Give examples (e.g., a teacher who discusses your future educational goals, a coach that works with you on your skill in a sport, an aunt or an uncle who is there to listen to you).

Being a Mentor

Explain in your own words:

Mentors can be older, but you can be a mentor regardless of your age.

Ask:

Who could you be a mentor to?

Write a list of responses on the board. List may include:

- friends
- younger relatives
- fellow classmates
- teammates
- neighborhood children

HANDOUT 3.2

Give each participant a copy of handout 3.2, "Mentoring."

Explain in your own words:

On the handout, write down what you would like a mentor to do for you. This will help you to think about who might be good mentors for you. Then write down what you might do to mentor someone.

Ask:

In what ways can you be a mentor? Or, what qualifications do you have that would make you a good mentor to someone? You can also write down who you would like to mentor at the bottom of the handout.

After the participants complete the list, encourage them to share some responses with other participants.

Explain:

One traditional Native belief tells us:

TRADITIONAL
NATIVE BELIEF

"All things are interrelated and all things have life (spiritual energy). Everything is part of a whole and each element in the universe has its place and its function. Hence, all things are worthy of respect and reverence. The sacred relationship we have with the universe is to be honored."

Ask:

How does this traditional belief apply to communities?

Allow for responses.

Club Drugs and Stimulants

In this section, participants identify the adverse effects of club drugs and stimulants.

Explain in your own words:

One way to honor our sacred relationship with the universe is to avoid the use of drugs, including "club drugs" and stimulants. Let's form two groups for a relay race. We will race for facts about these drugs.

Form two groups and, if needed, ask them to sit together.

Pass out copies of handout 3.3, "Club Drugs," to the first group and handout 3.4, "Stimulants," to the second group.

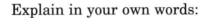

HANDOUT 3.3

Then give the first group one copy of handout 3.5, and the second group one copy of handout 3.6. They will use these worksheets to answer your questions, one at a time.

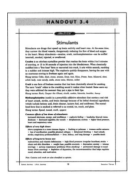

HANDOUT 3.4

HANDOUT 3.5   HANDOUT 3.6

Explain to all participants:

I will give each group one question at a time. The group will find the correct answer on their handout, write the answer down, and pass it to me. I'll tell them if the answer is right, and if it is, the group can go on to the next question. If it's wrong, the group tries again. The two groups will be working at the same time. The team that answers all the questions correctly in the fastest time will win the relay.

> ▶ **Facilitator Tip**
> See pages 74–75 for the questions you will ask and the answers to expect. You can either ask the questions out loud (one at a time), or write them down in advance on slips of paper and hand them in sequence to each group.

After the relay race, discuss any questions or issues that come up.

Then ask:

Would we want to take club drugs or stimulants on a canoe journey?

Allow for responses.

Explain:

So that leads to the question that each of us should ask ourselves: "Do I want club drugs or stimulants to be a part of my life's journey?"

Conclusion

HANDOUT 3.7

Here we summarize what has been learned throughout this session using the Medicine Wheel.

Give each participant a copy of handout 3.7, "What Did You Learn?"

Draw a Medicine Wheel on the board.

Ask:

Using the Medicine Wheel's four dimensions, what could we say that we have learned in this session?

Allow for responses. Generate responses and include some of the following if the participants can't come up with their own.

Mental

- I have learned the importance of community.
- I have learned about the communities around me.
- I have learned that I'm a part of many communities.
- I have learned about the qualities of a good mentor and how to become one.

Spiritual

- Working together in a community can help us with our spiritual journey through life.
- Each of us has our own spiritual journey.
- Having others along on our spiritual journey makes it more meaningful.

Physical

- I see the importance of getting out and participating with others in my community.
- I know the benefits resulting from being a part of many communities.

Emotional

- I understand the importance of feeling supported and cared for in our community.
- I learned how we can support and care for others in return.
- I can see how a mentor impacts our emotional well-being.
- I understand the comfort of having someone to turn to in time of need.

Ask each participant to share an item or two from the handout. Ask questions to prompt discussion.

> ▶ **Facilitator Tip**
> Participants should be given time to complete the handout during the session. Do not allow participants to take the assignments home.

Duplicating this page is illegal. Do not copy without publisher's written permission.

73

Facilitator Q and A: Club Drugs

QUESTIONS	ANSWERS
1. What is Ketamine?	A fast-acting painkiller (injected, snorted, or smoked) that produces a dissociative high.
2. What is Rohypnol commonly called?	The "date-rape" drug.
3. What are the immediate effects of MDMA (Ecstasy)?	Feelings such as euphoria, relaxation, enhanced sensations, empathy, self-acceptance. Also lifts blood pressure and heart rate.
4. What are four slang terms for Rohypnol?	Roofies, R-2, circles, Mexican Valium, roach-2, roopies. (Also known as a date-rape drug.)
5. What are some adverse effects of Ketamine?	High blood pressure, amnesia, seizures, respiratory depression, impaired motor function.
6. What are some adverse effects of GHB?	Nausea, loss of consciousness, drowsiness, respiratory distress, dizziness, seizures, inability to remember what happened during the hours after use.
7. What are club drugs?	Illegal drugs often used at nightclubs, concerts, and parties. They include stimulants, depressants, and hallucinogens.
8. Why is it often impossible to know the ingredients of a club drug?	They are often made in makeshift laboratories.
9. What are the adverse effects of Ecstasy?	Heart and kidney damage; long-term injury to areas of the brain critical to thought and memory.
10. What brain chemical is released by Ecstasy?	Serotonin.

Facilitator Q and A: Stimulants

QUESTIONS	ANSWERS
1. What are four slang terms for methamphetamine?	Speed, tweak, meth, uppers.
2. What is the difference between crack and cocaine?	Cocaine is snorted or injected; crack is a form of freebase cocaine that can be smoked.
3. What are three common stimulants?	Cocaine, crack, and methamphetamine.
4. What are some of the chemical products used to make meth?	Battery acid, drain cleaner, lantern fuel, and antifreeze, among others.
5. How addictive is crack?	Highly addictive. Some say they were addicted from the moment they tried it.
6. How quickly does cocaine reach the brain if snorted?	In about 3 to 5 minutes.
7. In what ways can stimulants be ingested?	Many of them can be sniffed (snorted), smoked, injected, or swallowed.
8. What is the effect of chemically modifying cocaine into a "free base" form?	It works faster, reaching the brain in seconds.
9. What are four slang terms for cocaine?	Any of these terms: coke, dust, snow, sneeze, lines, toot, blow, freeze, base, blizzard, sleet, white lady, nose candy, soda, snow cone, blanco, cubes.
10. What are three kinds of major medical problems caused by the chemical ingredients in meth?	Heart attack, stroke, and serious brain damage.

The Communities Around You

Can you think of some different communities you are a part of?

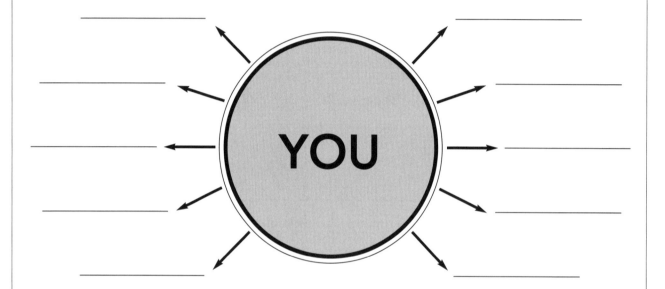

What are things you need to know or skills you need to have
in order to do well in other communities?

_____

_____

_____

_____

_____

_____

_____

_____

Mentoring

My mentor will . . .	I can be a mentor by . . .

Club Drugs

Often used at nightclubs, concerts, and raves (all-night dance parties), club drugs include stimulants, depressants, and hallucinogens. They can be smoked, snorted, injected, or swallowed. These drugs can damage the brain and impair senses, memory, judgment, and coordination. Because club drugs are illegal and often produced in unsanitary makeshift labs, users rarely know what chemicals went into the drug, or exactly how strong or dangerous it is. It varies every time. Some common club drugs are listed here.

MDMA ("Ecstasy") causes a relaxed and euphoric state. The user feels enhanced sensations, emotional warmth, and self-acceptance. Both a stimulant and a hallucinogen, MDMA releases the brain chemical serotonin, which lifts mood, blood pressure, and heart rate. Use can lead to heart or kidney damage and brain injury that compromises thinking and memory.

Slang terms: *E, X, XTC, M, Adam, bean, roll*

Ketamine is a fast-acting painkiller that is injected, snorted, or smoked. Ketamine produces a dissociative state—a feeling of detachment from surroundings—and can even elicit an out-of-body experience. Adverse effects include high blood pressure, amnesia, seizures, respiratory depression and impaired motor function.

Slang terms: *K, Special K, Ket, Vitamin K, Kit Kat*

Rohypnol, a sedative, is commonly called the "date rape" drug. While usually in pill form, it can also be an odorless powder that can be put in someone's drink without them knowing. Adverse effects include decreased blood pressure, memory and vision impairment, drowsiness, dizziness, confusion, gastrointestinal pain, and sometimes aggressiveness.

Slang terms: *Roofies, R-2, circles, Mexican Valium, roach-2, roopies*

GHB is another date rape drug. Initially, its effects are like alcohol's: euphoria, relaxation, and calm. Adverse effects include nausea, loss of consciousness, drowsiness, respiratory distress, dizziness, and seizures. One risky symptom is forgetting what happened during the hours after ingesting it.

Slang terms: *Liquid ecstasy, liquid X, soap, cherry meth, Nature's Quaalude*

Note: The club drug methamphetamine ("meth") is discussed in handout 3.4,"Stimulants."

Stimulants

Stimulants are drugs that speed up brain activity and heart rate. At the same time, they narrow the blood vessels, dangerously reducing the flow of blood and oxygen to the heart. Many stimulants—cocaine, crack, methamphetamine—can be sniffed (snorted), smoked, injected, or swallowed.

Cocaine is an odorless crystalline powder that reaches the brain within 3 to 5 minutes of snorting, or 15 to 30 seconds of injection into the bloodstream. When chemically modified into a "free base" form or converted into crack, it acts within seconds, resulting in a sudden and intense high. The euphoria quickly disappears, leaving the user with an enormous craving to freebase again and again.
Slang terms: *Coke, dust, snow, sneeze, lines, toot, blow, freeze, base, blizzard, sleet, white lady, nose candy, soda, snow cone, blanco, cubes*

Crack is one form of freebase cocaine that has been chemically altered for smoking. The term "crack" refers to the crackling sound it makes when heated. Some users say they were addicted the moment they put a pipe to their lips.
Slang terms: *Rock, Casper the Ghost, chalk, cookie, biscuits, boulder, bump*

Methamphetamine (meth) is a powerfully addictive stimulant that carries a real risk of heart attack, stroke, and brain damage because of its lethal chemical ingredients (which include battery acid, drain cleaner, lantern fuel, and antifreeze). The crystallized form that is smoked is referred to as crystal, ice, crank, and glass.
Slang terms: *Speed, tweak, meth, uppers*

Common effects of low doses of stimulants:
   increased alertness, energy, and confidence • euphoric feeling • headache; blurred vision; dizziness • decreased appetite; dry mouth • sleeplessness; anxiety • higher blood pressure, heart and respiratory rates

Effects of very high doses:
   above symptoms to a more intense degree • flushing or paleness • tremors and/or seizures • loss of coordination; possible physical collapse • delusional thinking • heart attack; stroke; respiratory problems/failure • liver, kidney, and lung damage • possible death

Effects of long-term heavy use:
   malnutrition and vitamin deficiencies • high blood pressure: irregular heartbeat; stroke • ulcers and skin disorders • weight loss; possible anorexia • depression; anxiety • intense cravings • serious respiratory problems (from smoking) • permanent damage to nasal tissue (from snorting) • depletion of dopamine, the neurotransmitter that helps regulate mood, attention, and motivation

Note: Cocaine and crack are also classified as opiates.

Club Drugs Worksheet

1. _____

2. _____

3. _____

4. _____

5. _____

6. _____

7. _____

8. _____

9. _____

10. _____

Stimulants Worksheet

1.

2.

3.

4.

5.

6.

7.

8.

9.

10.

What Did You Learn?

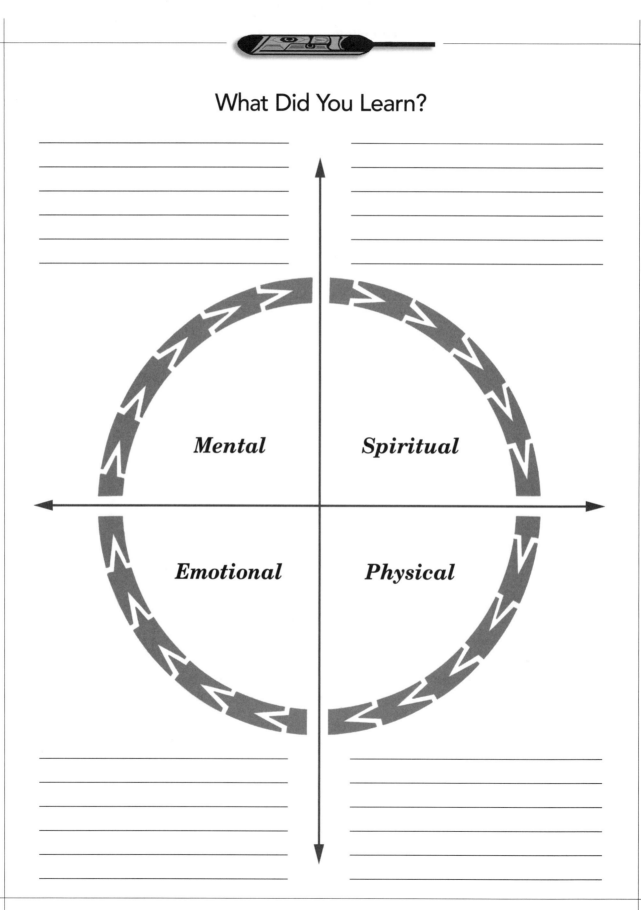

Mental

Spiritual

Emotional

Physical

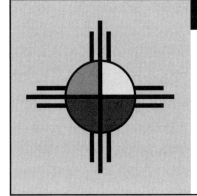

The Quest

GOAL SETTING

Purpose of Session 4

In this session participants learn the skills necessary to set goals, plan those goals, and then examine the steps it will take to reach them. Participants will also see how drugs such as hallucinogens can interfere with these goals.

Learner Outcomes

By the end of this session, participants will be able to:

- determine what kinds of goals are important
- identify a step-by-step approach to setting goals
- define the importance of goal setting
- identify ways to cope with obstacles—such as drugs—that may hinder achieving goals

Materials Needed

- ☐ flip chart, white board, or chalk board
- ☐ markers or chalk
- ☐ poster board
- ☐ masking tape
- ☐ handout 4.1, *Goal Setting and Planning*
- ☐ handout 4.2, *What Do You Know About Hallucinogens?*
- ☐ handout 4.3, *Hallucinogens*
- ☐ handout 4.4, *What Did You Learn?*

Preparation Needed

1. Read session 4 in its entirety to become familiar with it.

2. If you've provided binders or folders for participants, bring them along to distribute at the start of the session.

3. Photocopy all handouts and hole-punch if needed. Handouts appear in this book after each session outline; they can also be printed from the CD-ROM (if using a color printer, decorative elements will appear in color). During the session, distribute them one by one as prompted.

4. Arrange the room so that each participant can be included in the conversation.

5. If you created ground rules in session 1, post them for all participants to view.

Goal Setting

In this session, participants set some goals and then make some concrete plans for achieving those goals. Participants will learn the five steps in goal setting:

- Plan: Define and plan the goal
- Do it
- Check your progress
- Act
- Celebrate!

Explain in your own words:

We often daydream about what the future holds for us. Fantasy and imagination are fun because there are no limits to what we can imagine for ourselves.

Ask:

What are some dreams that you have had?

Allow for responses and then write them on the board or flip chart.

Ask:

Where would you like to see yourself in the next few weeks, next few months, next few years?

Allow for responses and then write them on the board or flip chart.

> ▶ **Facilitator Tip**
> If the participants are reluctant to respond, give them a personal example of your own dreams and goals to help get them started.

Ask:

Why is it important to have goals and to make plans to achieve them?

Allow for responses.

TRADITIONAL

NATIVE BELIEF

Explain:

One traditional Native belief says that:

"The spiritual dimension of human development consists of four areas: visions, ideals, dreams, and goals. Having the experience of any of these symbolizes a need for change and they serve as a guide to future behavior."

Having a goal is an expression of our spiritual dimension and it means that we need to actively work toward reaching our goals. Goals are like dreams, but they are more detailed and planned. In order to achieve our dreams or goals, there are several things we need to consider. We need to:

- **identify what we want**

- **decide how we will reach our goals**

- **determine the smaller steps we must take to achieve our bigger goals**

- **ponder what kinds of things are important to us and what we value**

- **identify what obstacles may hinder progress toward reaching our goals**

HANDOUT 4.1

Give each participant a copy of handout 4.1, "Goal Setting and Planning."

Explain:

This session is about setting goals, goal planning, and examining the steps it will take to reach your goals. Let's use the canoe journey as an example for following these steps.

Goals for a Canoe Journey: Five Steps

Ask:

What are some goals related to an actual canoe journey?

Allow for responses. Possible responses may include:

- to prepare physically for the journey

- to prepare emotionally for the journey

- to complete the journey successfully

- to stay alive to complete the journey

After the participants have come up with a list, review the possible answers listed above and suggest any they might have missed.

Explain in your own words:

It's time to make a plan. Let's define those goals and make a plan for achieving them, using five steps.

Step 1　　**Step 1 is "Define and plan the goal." As an example, let's select the goal "To prepare physically for the journey" and go through the four remaining steps in goal setting.**

Ask each of the following questions and generate responses for each:

- **Why do you think being physically fit for the journey is important?**
- **How will you accomplish the goal of getting in shape for the journey?**
- **Where would you go to get physically fit for the journey?**
- **Who will help you to get fit?**
- **When will you start working on getting physically fit?**
- **What are some obstacles that may hinder your progress toward reaching your goal?**

Explain the remaining goal-setting steps:

Step 2　　**Step 2 is "Do it": Follow through with the plan for completing the journey.**

Step 3　　**Step 3 is "Check your progress":**
- **Are you on schedule?**
- **Do you have all the necessary resources?**
- **Do you need to change any part of your original plan?**

Step 4　　**Step 4 is "Act": Make any necessary changes and continue with your plan or assess the situation to decide if you should change course.**

Duplicating this page is illegal. Do not copy without publisher's written permission.

87

Step 5

Step 5 is "Celebrate"! This is the last thing you should do after reaching a goal. You should also celebrate while you are making progress. Celebrating—commemorating benchmarks or major events—is a traditional way of honoring events or necessary changes.

Explain in your own words:

Goals are usually not reached without going through all of the steps in the middle. One way to accomplish a larger goal is to set smaller goals and intermediate goals.

**Smaller
Goals**

Ask:

Why do you think setting smaller goals will be helpful?

Generate responses. The list may include:

- We might not have the dedication without the smaller goals.
- We might feel overwhelmed by having only long-term goals.
- With smaller goals and steps you can see your progress.
- Smaller steps make the goal seem possible to achieve.

After the participants have come up with a list, suggest any important ones they might have missed.

Ask:

On an actual canoe journey, what smaller goals might be set to achieve the final destination?

Generate responses. The list may include:

- to get to that day's destination
- to paddle until the next meal
- to become better in working as a team
- to spend time thinking or focusing on oneself

After the participants have come up with a list, suggest any important ones they might have missed.

Explain in your own words:

Remember to look at the distance you have traveled, not only at the distance left to go. Always take note of your progress!

Obstacles on the Journey

In this discussion participants examine some obstacles that might get in the way of achieving some set goals. These obstacles will include taking along or using drugs like hallucinogens.

Explain:

One more thing that needs to be considered in examining goals: the obstacles that might prevent you from reaching them.

Ask:

What are some obstacles that might hinder progress in reaching goals?

Generate responses and write them on the board. The list may include:

- drugs and alcohol
- lack of focus
- bad relationships

After the participants have come up with a list, suggest any they might have missed.

Explain in your own words:

Keeping these kinds of pitfalls in mind will help you avoid them.

Hallucinogens

HANDOUT 4.2

HANDOUT 4.3

Explain in your own words:

One potential obstacle that would interfere with a successful canoe journey is the use of drugs and alcohol. We will look at hallucinogens in this session. Before we distribute the next handout, let's see how much you already know about hallucinogens.

Distribute handout 4.2, "What Do You Know about Hallucinogens?" and allow time for them to complete it.

Briefly review the handout aloud to check participants' general level of knowledge. If they don't know very much about hallucinogens, applaud them for that. If they have accurate knowledge about them (perhaps from a health class), validate what they know.

Give each participant a copy of handout 4.3, "Hallucinogens," and briefly review the content, pointing out the answers to the questions on the previous handout.

Then ask:

Would we want to take hallucinogens on a canoe journey?

Allow for responses.

Explain in your own words:

That leads to the question that each of us should ask ourselves: "Do I want hallucinogens to be a part of my life's journey?"

Conclusion

HANDOUT 4.4

In this section, participants summarize what has been learned throughout this session using the Medicine Wheel.

Give each participant a copy of handout 4.4, "What Did You Learn?"

Draw a Medicine Wheel on the board.

Ask:

Using the Medicine Wheel's four dimensions, what could we say we have learned in this session?

Allow for responses. Generate responses and include some of the following if the participants can't come up with their own.

Mental

- I have learned the importance of setting goals.
- I have learned the steps involved in goal setting.
- I have learned how to maneuver around obstacles that may prevent me from reaching my goal.
- I now know that both short-term and intermediate goals can help me reach my long-term goals.

Spiritual

- I realize that my dreams and hopes for the future help me define my goals.
- Examining our spiritual motivation affects how we reach our goals.

Physical

- Setting goals involves physical activity.
- Being active helps us set and achieve goals.

Emotional

- It's wise to examine our motivations in goal setting.
- Balance is important in accomplishing goals.
- Determination has an impact on achieving goals.

Ask each participant to share an item or two from the handout. Ask questions to spark discussion.

> ▶ **Facilitator Tip**
> Participants should be given time to complete the handout during the session. Do not allow participants to take the assignments home.

Duplicating this page is illegal. Do not copy without publisher's written permission.

91

Goal Setting and Planning

Define and plan the goal: Ask the *What*, *When*, *Where*, *Who*, *Why*, and *How* questions.

Do it: Execute the plan.

Check your progress: Are you on schedule? Do you have all the necessary resources? Do you need to change any part of your original plan?

Act on your revised plan: Make any necessary changes and continue with your plan. Or assess the situation to decide if you should change your course.

What is the goal?

When can you carry out this goal?

Where can you carry out this goal?

Who is involved in carrying out the plan?

Why is this goal important to you?

How will you carry out the plan to reach your goal?

What are the obstacles that might hinder your progress toward meeting your goals?

What are some goals that you now have?

What Do You Know About Hallucinogens?

❶ What are hallucinogens?

❷ What are some effects of hallucinogens?

❸ What are dissociative drugs?

❹ What is PCP?

❺ Is Ecstasy a hallucinogen? __ Yes __ No

❻ Why are hallucinogens dangerous?

❼ What is a flashback?

❽ What is a "bad trip"?

❾ Which of the five senses do hallucinogens affect (sight, hearing, touch, taste, smell)?

❿ How long does an LSD trip last?

Hallucinogens

Hallucinogens are drugs that act on the central nervous system to produce altered states of perception, feeling, and consciousness. They can change how the brain perceives everyday reality, the environment, and time. Hallucinogens affect regions of the brain responsible for sight, hearing, coordination, and thought processes. Users often see or hear things that aren't really there. Some hallucinogens also produce rapid, intense emotional swings.

Also known as "psychedelic" drugs, they include LSD, "magic mushrooms," mescaline, PCP (phencyclidine), and marijuana. Marijuana is a depressant as well as a hallucinogen. (Some of these drugs appear on other session handouts, too.)

What are the effects of hallucinogen use?

LSD and other hallucinogens such as MDMA (Ecstasy) and PCP produce a wide range of changes in thought, perceptions, and behavior in users, often affecting all five senses. A "normal" LSD trip starts 30 to 90 minutes after ingestion and may last twelve hours. The initial physical effects include nausea, dizziness, dilated pupils, muscle weakness, and loss of appetite.

Slang terms for some hallucinogens:

Ketamine (a common club drug): *K, Special K, Vitamin K, Kit Kat, Kelly's Day, blind squid, Cat Valium, super acid.*

MDMA ("Ecstasy," another club drug): *E, X, XTC, M, Adam, bean, roll.*

Lysergic acid diethylamide: *LSD, acid, blotter.*

Phencyclidine: *PCP, angel dust, loveboat, boat, ozone, wack.*

Psilocybin: *Mushrooms, shrooms, magics.*

CONTINUED ON NEXT PAGE

What are dissociative drugs?

Many hallucinogens can have "dissociative" effects on the user. Dissociative drugs provide mind-altering effects that give a feeling of detachment from self and environment. They distort vision and hearing and can initiate "out-of-body" or "near-death" experiences. They act by altering the brain's distribution of the neurotransmitter glutamate, which affects perception of pain, responses to the environment, and memory. The effects of dissociative drugs include numbness, loss of coordination, a sense of great strength and invulnerability, muscle rigidity, aggressive and violent behavior, slurred or blocked speech, and an inhibited respiratory system.

Adverse effects of hallucinogens:

- The drugs often induce feelings of panic.

- The user may experience "flashbacks" at any time, during or after use.

- Hallucinations have caused users to behave in ways that endanger their lives and may even cause death (for example, users jump from high windows because they think they can fly).

- There is risk of a "bad trip," depending on the strength and purity of the drug and on the user's frame of mind.

- Common effects are increased heart rate and blood pressure, irregular breathing, inability to reason and to separate fact from fantasy, paranoia, violence, and rapid mood swings.

What Did You Learn?

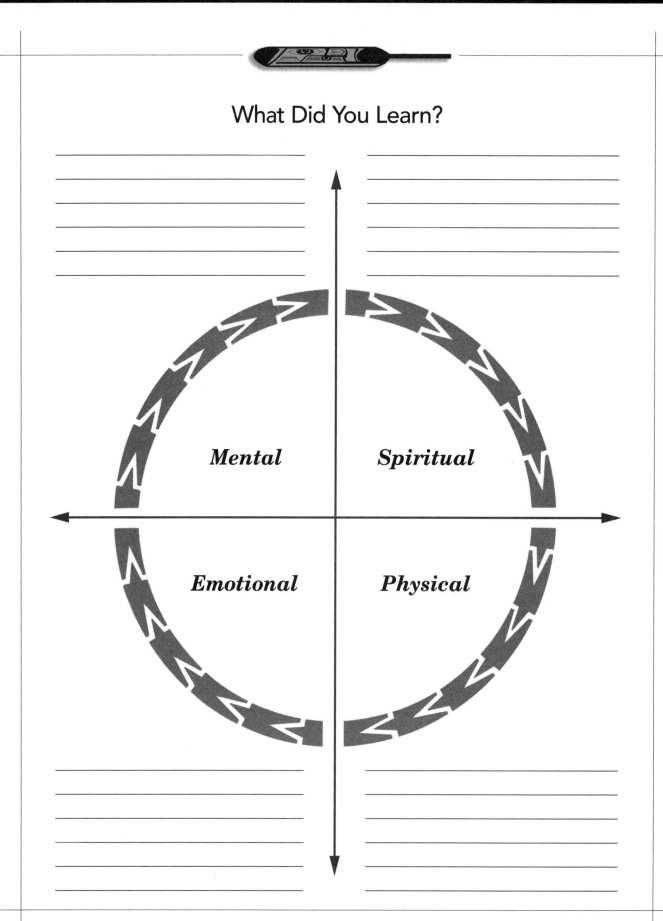

Mental

Spiritual

Emotional

Physical

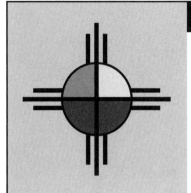

Overcoming Obstacles

SOLVING PROBLEMS

Purpose of Session 5

In this session participants learn the six skills needed to solve problems. A Native story will be told about Veeho, a coyote who made some poor decisions, with disastrous results. It will also focus on nicotine and explain how this can create more problems for us.

Learner Outcomes

By the end of this session, participants will be able to:

- recognize when they are having a problem
- identify ways to solve those problems
- identify problem solving approaches
- determine how to make good decisions
- explain how nicotine can be an obstacle to healthy living

Materials Needed

- ☐ flip chart, white board, or chalk board
- ☐ markers or chalk
- ☐ handout 5.1, *Six Steps to Problem Solving*
- ☐ handout 5.2, *Problems on Life's Journey*
- ☐ handout 5.3, *Doing a Trick with Eyeballs*
- ☐ handout 5.4, *What Do You Know About Nicotine?*
- ☐ handout 5.5, *Nicotine*
- ☐ handout 5.6, *What Did You Learn?*

Preparation Needed

1. Read session 5 in its entirety to become familiar with it.

2. Reflect on the story *Doing a Trick with Eyeballs* (also in handout 5.3). Be prepared to retell it in your own words, or to read it out loud if you prefer.

3. If you've provided binders or folders for participants, bring them along to distribute at the start of the session.

4. Photocopy all handouts and hole-punch if needed. Handouts appear in this book after each session outline; they can also be printed from the CD-ROM (if using a color printer, decorative elements will appear in color). During the session, distribute them one by one as prompted.

5. Arrange the room so that each participant can be included in the conversation.

6. If you created ground rules in session 1, post them for all participants to view.

More Obstacles on the Journey

In this session, participants explore further obstacles on the canoe journey and determine how to deal with these obstacles. They also discover a six-step process to help people deal with any kind of obstacle encountered in life.

Solving Problems on a Canoe Journey

Explain in your own words:

Let's go back to our theme of the canoe journey. Each day before the pullers place their canoes in the water, prayers are said to ask for a safe and problem-free trip.

Ask:

What are some of the obstacles that can be encountered on a canoe journey?

Generate a list of obstacles and write them on the board. The list may include:

- a leak in the boat
- people not getting along
- losing our way
- too much rain or too much sun
- people needing to go to the bathroom at awkward times

Ask:

And why do you think having a strategy for problem solving would be helpful?

Allow for responses.

Explain in your own words:

In real life, people often make choices out of habit without going through the decision-making steps systematically. They are more likely to rely on personal experience. Often decisions are made under social pressure or time constraints that interfere with a careful consideration of the options and consequences. When people lack adequate information or skills, they may make less than optimal decisions.

Having these problem-solving steps will help you avoid the pitfalls of poor decision making.

Duplicating this page is illegal. Do not copy without publisher's written permission.

99

Explain:

The following traditional Native belief applies to problem solving:

"Human beings have the ability to learn new skills, but they must be willing to do so through life lessons and elder teachings."

Ask:

How does this Native belief apply to problem solving?

Allow for responses.

Six Steps to Problem Solving

HANDOUT 5.1

Explain:

We are going to share with you a structured and efficient way to solve problems.

Give each participant a copy of handout 5.1, "Six Steps to Problem Solving."

> ▶ **Facilitator Note**
> Be thoroughly familiar with the handout's six steps.
> *Optional:* select several participants to help you read aloud each step.

Explain the handout by reviewing each step.

Step 1 is "Define the problem." So let's define our problem, and let's be very specific and detailed. You must have the problem clearly defined in order to come up with a good solution.

Let's look at the problem "Having a leak in the canoe."

Ask:

So what else might be important in defining this problem?

Explain:

Ask yourself the following questions:

- **Where is the leak?**

- **How big is the leak?**
- **Is it a big enough problem to address?**
- **How immediately serious is the problem?**

Allow for responses. You may choose to write down participant responses on the board or flip chart.

Explain:

Step 2 is "Brainstorm Solutions." So let's think out loud. Include any ideas, even if they are outlandish and don't make sense. When your mind is free enough to think of crazy ideas, it is then free enough to think of new practical, sensible ideas.

Brainstorm solutions for a leak in the canoe.

Ask the participants to think of possible solutions and then write them on the board or flip chart. Solutions may include:

- Plug it up with chewing gum.
- Stop and jump into the water to patch it.
- Take the canoe on shore, then fix it.
- Have someone stick a finger in the hole.

To start brainstorming, you may review the possible answers listed above and suggest them.

Explain:

Step 3 is "Pick the solution that you think is best." Let's examine one of the solutions for a leak in the canoe. Solution A is "Plug the hole up with chewing gum." So let's look at the idea carefully and ask yourself the following questions regarding plugging up the hole with chewing gum.

Ask each of the following questions and then allow enough time for a variety of responses:

- **What are the consequences associated with this solution?**
- **What will happen if you use this solution?**
- **Is the solution practical?**

Duplicating this page is illegal. Do not copy without publisher's written permission.

101

- **Does the solution get you what you want?**
- **Are there any problems associated with this solution?**
- **What effect will this solution have on others?**
- **What is involved in the process of carrying out the solution?**
- **How much will it cost?**
- **How long will it take to carry out the solution?**
- **How much energy will it take to carry out the solution?**
- **Who else is needed to carry out the solution?**

If time allows, examine some of the other solutions and go through the questions listed above.

- Solution B: Stop, jump into the water, and patch it.
- Solution C: Take the canoe on shore, then fix it.
- Solution D: Have someone stick a finger in the hole.

Explain:

Step 4 is "Make a plan based on this solution." Ask yourself the following questions regarding the solution "Plugging the hole with chewing gum."

- **What should I do first?**
- **Whose help is needed?**
- **What is the best way to carry the idea through?**
- **How much time should I give the solution to work before I decide to ditch the idea?**

Allow time for responses.

Explain:

Step 5 is "Act on it." Follow the first solution you have selected: Plug the hole with chewing gum.

Explain:

Step 6 is "Review and revise your plan."

- **If your plan didn't work, what went wrong?**
- **If your plan did work, remember that too.**
- **If your first plan didn't work, you have a list of ideas to work from.**

Solving Real-Life Problems

Here, participants apply these problem-solving skills to real-life problems.

Explain and ask:

Now that we solved some problems that may occur on the canoe journey, let's use the six steps to solve some real-life problems. Can you think of a real-life problem that we might apply the problem-solving skills to?

Generate a few "problem situations" and write them on the board.

Explain:

Let's form groups of three for this exercise in problem-solving. We'll use the situations you've just described, and also a few from this handout.

Distribute handout 5.2, "Problems on Life's Journey," and assign each group one or two situations to solve.

Let the groups work together, using the six steps.

When all the groups have reached solutions, ask each group to briefly describe their problem situations, the solutions, and how the six-step process worked for them.

HANDOUT 5.2

A Story About Problem Solving

Explain in your own words:

Now I would like to tell a Native story called "Doing a Trick with Eyeballs" about Veeho the coyote. As I tell the story, think about whether the coyote is a good problem solver.

Give each participant a copy of handout 5.3, "Doing a Trick with Eyeballs."

> ▶ **Facilitator Tip**
> If there are two facilitators, one may choose to be the storyteller and one may choose to be the character Veeho.

HANDOUT 5.3

**Story:
*Doing a Trick
with Eyeballs***

Tell the story.

Veeho is like some tourists who come into an Indian village not knowing how to behave or what to do, trying to impress everybody. One day Veeho met a medicine man with great powers. This man thought to amuse Veeho—and himself—with a little trick.

"Eyeballs," he shouted, "I command you to fly out of my head and hang on that tree over there." At once his eyeballs shot out of his head and in a flash were hanging from a tree branch. Veeho watched open-mouthed.

"Ho! Eyeballs!" cried the medicine man. "Now come back where you belong!" And quick as lightning, the eyeballs were back where they ought to be.

"Uncle," said Veeho, "please give me a little of your power so that I too can do this wonderful trick." To himself Veeho was thinking, "Then I can set up as a medicine man; then people will look up to me, especially good-looking girls; then people will give me many gifts!"

"Why not?" said the medicine man. "Why not give you a little power to please you? But, listen, Veeho, don't do this trick more than four times a day, or your eyeballs won't come back."

"I won't," said Veeho.

Veeho could hardly wait to get away and try out this stunning trick. As soon as he was alone, he ordered: "Eyeballs, hop on that ledge over there. Jump to it!" And the eyeballs did. Veeho couldn't see a thing.

"Quickly, eyeballs, back into your sockets!" The eyeballs obeyed.

"Boy, oh boy," Veeho said to himself, "what a big man I am. Powerful, really powerful." Soon he saw another tree.

"Eyeballs, up into that tree, quick!" For a second time the eyeballs did as they were told.

"Back in the skull!" Veeho shouted, snapping his fingers. And once more the eyeballs jumped back. Veeho was enjoying

himself, getting used to this marvelous trick. He couldn't stop. Twice more he performed it.

"Well, that's it for today," he said.

Later he came to a big village and wanted to impress the people with his powers. "Would you believe it, cousins," he told them, "I can make my eyeballs jump out of my head, fly over to that tree, hang themselves from a branch, and come back when I tell them."

The people, of course, didn't believe him; they laughed. Veeho grew angry. "It's true, it's true!" he cried. "You stupid people, I can do it."

"Show us," said the people.

"How often have I done this trick?" Veeho tried to remember. "Four times? No, no. The first time was only for practice; it doesn't count. I can still show these dummies something." And he commanded: "Eyeballs, hang yourselves on a branch of that tree!" The eyeballs did, and a great cry of wonder and astonishment went up.

"There, you louts, didn't I tell you?" said Veeho, strutting around, puffing himself up. After a while he said: "All right, eyeballs, come back!" But the eyeballs stayed up in the tree.

"Come back, come back, you no-good eyeballs!" Veeho cried again and again, but the eyeballs stayed put.

Finally a big fat crow landed on the tree and gobbled them up. "Mm, good," said the crow, "very tasty." The people laughed at Veeho, shook their heads, and went away.

Veeho was blind now. He didn't know what to do. He groped through the forest. He stumbled. He ran into trees. He sat down by a stone and cried. He heard a squeaking sound. It was a mouse calling other mice.

"Mouse, little mouse," cried Veeho, "I am blind. Please lend me one of your eyes so that I can see again."

"My eyes are tiny," answered the mouse, "much too tiny. What good would one of them do you? It wouldn't fit."

Duplicating this page is illegal. Do not copy without publisher's written permission.

105

But Veeho begged so pitifully that the mouse finally gave him an eye, saying: "I guess I can get along with the other one."

So Veeho had one eye, but it was very small indeed. What he saw was just a tiny speck of light. Still, it was better than nothing. Veeho staggered on and met a buffalo.

"Buffalo brother," he begged, "I have to get along with just this one tiny mouse eye. How can a big man like me make do with that? Have pity on me, brother, and lend me one of your big, beautiful eyes."

"What good would one of my eyes do you?" asked the buffalo. "It's much too big for your eye hole."

But Veeho begged and wept and wheedled until the buffalo said: "Well, all right, I'll let you have one. I can't stand listening to you carrying on like that. I guess I can get by with one eye."

And so Veeho had his second eye. The buffalo bull's eye was much too big, it made everything look twice as big as his own eyes had. And since the mouse eye saw everything ten times smaller, Veeho got a bad headache. But what could he do? It was better than being blind. "It's a bad mess, though," said Veeho.

Veeho went back to his wife and lodge. His wife looked at him. "I believe your eyes are a little mismatched," she told him. And he described all that had happened to him. "You know," she said, "I think you should stop fooling around, trying to impress people with tricks."

Ask:

Did coyote have good or bad problem-solving skills?

Explain in your own words:

It's obvious that coyote was not an active participant in making changes in his life and he did not use a systematic, well-thought-out approach to problem solving. He brought problems onto himself and made them worse by continuing to make bad decisions.

Nicotine

HANDOUT 5.4

HANDOUT 5.5

In this discussion, participants focus on nicotine and explain how this drug can cause problems for us.

Explain in your own words:

Life will always give us problems, and we can solve them thoughtfully and creatively. But why would we go looking for extra problems—like the health problems caused by using nicotine? Let's look at nicotine. How much do you already know about it?

Distribute handout 5.4, "What Do You Know About Nicotine?" and say:

This is a true-or-false questionnaire. Take a few minutes to fill it out, then we'll discuss it.

Then give each participant a copy of handout 5.5, "Nicotine," and briefly review the contents, pointing out the answers to the questions on the previous handout.

Correct answers are shown below.

1. True	5. True	8. True
2. False	6. True	9. False
3. True	7. True	10. True
4. False		

Ask:

Would we want to take nicotine on a canoe journey?

Allow for responses.

Ask:

But what about using tobacco ceremonially?

Explain in your own words:

Many Natives use tobacco because it is a sacred herb that is used for purification and healing.

Ask:

But how is using it ceremonially different from using it as a drug?

Allow for responses.

Explain in your own words:

The ceremonial use of tobacco occurs only on special occasions and not on a daily basis.

So that leads to the question that each of us should ask ourselves: "Do I want nicotine to be a part of my life's journey?"

Conclusion

HANDOUT 5.6

Here, participants summarize what has been learned throughout this session using the Medicine Wheel.

Give each participant a copy of handout 5.6, "What Did You Learn?" and briefly review the contents.

Draw a Medicine Wheel on the board.

Ask:

Using the Medicine Wheel's four dimensions, what could we say that we have learned in this session?

Allow for responses. Suggest some of the following if the participants can't come up with their own. Possible answers might include:

Mental

- I have learned to problem solve systematically.
- I have learned how brainstorming can help me find solutions.
- I have learned how to apply the steps to solve real life problems.
- I now know that it takes time and effort to problem solve.

Spiritual

- I honor the Creator for giving me the power to problem solve.
- My spiritual nature helps me cope with my problems.
- Asking the Creator for guidance in problem solving is a good thing.

Physical

- Problem solving can involve physical activity.
- Endurance, stamina, and inner strength all play a part in problem solving.
- A lack of problem-solving skills can be detrimental to our physical health.

Emotional

- We can avoid pitfalls by following a systematic plan instead of just basing decisions on out-of-control emotions and poor judgment.
- I am confident in my decision when I use the problem-solving skills that I've learned.

Ask each participant to share an item or two from the handout. Ask questions to spark discussion.

> ▶ **Facilitator Tip**
> Participants should be given time to complete the handout during the session. Do not allow participants to take the assignments home.

Six Steps to Problem Solving

1. Define the problem.

2. Brainstorm solutions.

3. Pick the best solution.

4. Make a plan.

5. Act on the plan.

6. Review and revise your plan.

Problems on Life's Journey

Life Problem 1: You are on the canoe journey. Another person on the journey, who used to be your friend, is now bullying you constantly. You don't want to tell anyone because you don't want to be known as a "snitch," but you are being harassed every day. What should you do?

Life Problem 2: You are on the canoe journey. A person who used to be your best friend is no longer speaking to you. Now that person is spreading ugly rumors about you to other young people on the journey. Hardly anyone is talking to you and you suspect that it's because of the rumors. What should you do?

Life Problem 3: Your mother just told you that she is going to leave your father. You've known that your parents have been unhappy for a long time, but you didn't think they would separate. Your mother gives you the choice to go with her or stay with your father. You feel very torn between your parents. You love them both. What should you do?

Life Problem 4: Your friend drives to your house to pick you up to go to a party. You can tell that he has been drinking, and you are not comfortable getting in a car with him. You ask him to come into your house for a minute. This gives you the time to think of what to do. What should you do?

Life Problem 5: You and your best friend go to the mall. As you are looking through a store, you notice your friend stuffing clothes in her jacket. You didn't know that she was planning to shoplift, and you don't want to be a part of it. What should you do?

Life Problem 6: You have a friend you are really worried about. He recently told you he just broke up with his girlfriend and he's very depressed. He also told you he's thinking about suicide. He makes you promise not to tell anyone. What should you do?

Doing a Trick with Eyeballs

Veeho is like some tourists who come into an Indian village not knowing how to behave or what to do, trying to impress everybody. One day Veeho met a medicine man with great powers. This man thought to amuse Veeho—and himself—with a little trick.

"Eyeballs," he shouted, "I command you to fly out of my head and hang on that tree over there." At once his eyeballs shot out of his head and in a flash were hanging from a tree branch. Veeho watched open-mouthed.

"Ho! Eyeballs!" cried the medicine man. "Now come back where you belong!" And quick as lightning, the eyeballs were back where they ought to be.

"Uncle," said Veeho, "please give me a little of your power so that I too can do this wonderful trick." To himself Veeho was thinking, "Then I can set up as a medicine man; then people will look up to me, especially good-looking girls; then people will give me many gifts!"

"Why not?" said the medicine man. "Why not give you a little power to please you? But, listen, Veeho, don't do this trick more than four times a day, or your eyeballs won't come back."

"I won't," said Veeho. Veeho could hardly wait to get away and try out this stunning trick. As soon as he was alone, he ordered: "Eyeballs, hop on that ledge over there. Jump to it!" And the eyeballs did. Veeho couldn't see a thing.

"Quickly, eyeballs, back into your sockets!" The eyeballs obeyed.

"Boy, oh boy," Veeho said to himself, "what a big man I am. Powerful, really powerful." Soon he saw another tree.

"Eyeballs, up into that tree, quick!" For a second time the eyeballs did as they were told. "Back in the skull!" Veeho shouted, snapping his fingers. And once more the eyeballs jumped back. Veeho was enjoying himself, getting used to this marvelous trick. He couldn't stop. Twice more he performed it.

"Well, that's it for today," he said. Later he came to a big village and wanted to impress the people with his powers. "Would you believe it, cousins," he told them, "I can make my eyeballs jump out of my head, fly over to that tree, hang themselves from a branch, and come back when I tell them."

The people, of course, didn't believe him; they laughed. Veeho grew angry. "It's true, it's true!" he cried. "You stupid people, I can do it."

"Show us," said the people.

"How often have I done this trick?" Veeho tried to remember. "Four times? No, no. The first time was only for practice; it doesn't count. I can still show these dummies something." And he commanded: "Eyeballs, hang yourselves on a branch of that tree!" The eyeballs did, and a great cry of wonder and astonishment went up.

"There, you louts, didn't I tell you?" said Veeho, strutting around, puffing himself up. After a while he said: "All right, eyeballs, come back!" But the eyeballs stayed up in the tree. "Come back, come back, you no-good eyeballs!" Veeho cried again and again, but the eyeballs stayed put.

Finally a big fat crow landed on the tree and gobbled them up. "Mm, good," said the crow, "very tasty." The people laughed at Veeho, shook their heads, and went away.

Veeho was blind now. He didn't know what to do. He groped through the forest. He stumbled. He ran into trees. He sat down by a stone and cried. He heard a squeaking sound. It was a mouse calling other mice.

"Mouse, little mouse," cried Veeho, "I am blind. Please lend me one of your eyes so that I can see again."

"My eyes are tiny," answered the mouse, "much too tiny. What good would one of them do you? It wouldn't fit." But Veeho begged so pitifully that the mouse finally gave him an eye, saying: "I guess I can get along with the other one."

So Veeho had one eye, but it was very small indeed. What he saw was just a tiny speck of light. Still, it was better than nothing. Veeho staggered on and met a buffalo.

"Buffalo brother," he begged, "I have to get along with just this one tiny mouse eye. How can a big man like me make do with that? Have pity on me, brother, and lend me one of your big, beautiful eyes."

"What good would one of my eyes do you?" asked the buffalo. "It's much too big for your eye hole." But Veeho begged and wept and wheedled until the buffalo said, "Well, all right, I'll let you have one. I can't stand listening to you carrying on like that. I guess I can get by with one eye."

And so Veeho had his second eye. The buffalo bull's eye was much too big; it made everything look twice as big as his own eyes had. And since the mouse eye saw everything ten times smaller, Veeho got a bad headache. But what could he do? It was better than being blind. "It's a bad mess, though," said Veeho.

Veeho went back to his wife and lodge. His wife looked at him. "I believe your eyes are a little mismatched," she told him. And he described all that had happened to him. "You know," she said, "I think you should stop fooling around, trying to impress people with tricks."

What Do You Know About Nicotine?

Next to each statement, circle "**T**" for true or "**F**" for false.

❶ Tobacco smoke contains over 4,000 chemical compounds.   T   F

❷ Heavy nicotine users will never need more of the substance   T   F
to get the same effects.

❸ Nicotine increases alertness, concentration, and attention.   T   F

❹ Nicotine withdrawal symptoms do not occur until days after   T   F
the user's last fix.

❺ Chewing tobacco can cause cancer.   T   F

❻ Two tobacco withdrawal symptoms are nausea and vomiting.   T   F

❼ Smoking causes most lung cancer.   T   F

❽ A common household cleaner ingredient is also a compound   T   F
found in tobacco smoke.

❾ Smoking is cool.   T   F

❿ One early sign of oral cancer is a sore in the mouth that does   T   F
not heal.

Nicotine

Nicotine, a component of tobacco, is one of the United States' most heavily used addictive drugs. Cigarettes, chewing tobacco, and cigars all contain it.

Why is nicotine so addictive?

Nicotine causes the brain to release dopamine, which triggers the pleasure experienced by many smokers. Nicotine can act as a psychomotor stimulant, boost alertness and concentration, and reduce hunger. These effects draw users into repeated use. Nicotine tolerance occurs when the user needs larger amounts for the same effects. Ongoing (chronic) use produces tolerance and dependence in as little as a week!

According to the American Heart Association, in the United States, an estimated 25.5 million men (24.1 percent) and 21.5 million women (19.2 percent) are cigarette smokers.

What are the effects of smoking?

Smoking causes 87 percent of cases of lung cancer, says the American Lung Association. Smokers also have a higher risk of emphysema, bronchial disorders, and cardiovascular disease. Tobacco smoke contains over 4,000 chemical compounds, including carbon monoxide (like car exhaust fumes), formaldehyde (the substance used to preserve dead bodies), and ammonia (an ingredient in household cleaners). Nicotine can increase stomach acid, cause diarrhea, and raise heart rate and blood pressure.

What are the danger signs of smokeless tobacco?

Chewing tobacco causes cancer of the mouth, pharynx, larynx, and esophagus; gum damage, and tooth loss. If you have ever used smokeless tobacco, look for these early signs of oral cancer: a sore in the mouth that does not heal, a lump or white patch, a prolonged sore throat, difficulty in chewing, and/or restricted movement of the tongue or jaws.

What are the symptoms of withdrawal from nicotine?

Withdrawal occurs within several hours of the user's last "fix" and lasts about one week (which can make quitting difficult). Two or more of these symptoms typically develop:

intense cravings • sweating or rapid pulse • insomnia
physical agitation; hand tremors • irritability; anxiety • nausea or vomiting

What Did You Learn?

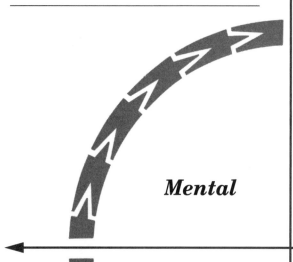
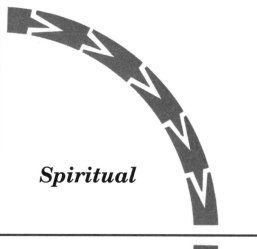
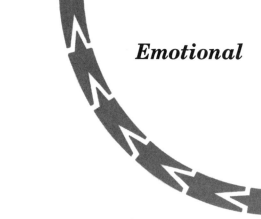

Mental

Spiritual

Emotional

Physical

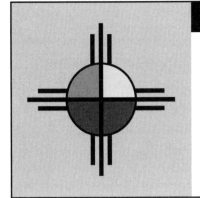

Effective Communication

LISTENING AND SELF-EXPRESSION

Purpose of Session 6

In this session, participants explore the important role communication plays in relationships. They will learn about different communication styles, the benefits of being assertive, how to be a good listener, and how feelings affect what they think, say, and do. Role-plays help build communication skills.

Learner Outcomes

By the end of this session, participants will be able to:

- understand the benefits of a positive communication style, both verbal and nonverbal

- realize that attentive listening lets the person talking know that she or he is important

- know the difference between aggressive, passive, and assertive communication styles

- confidently refuse to engage in harmful behaviors

- deal with potential peer reactions to assertiveness

- see how using opiates interferes with relationships

Duplicating this page is illegal. Do not copy without publisher's written permission.

117

Materials Needed

- ☐ flip chart, white board, or chalkboard
- ☐ markers or chalk
- ☐ handout 6.1, *Tips for Effective Listening*
- ☐ handout 6.2, *Three Ways to Express Feelings*
- ☐ handout 6.3, *Steps to Resolve Conflict*
- ☐ handout 6.4, *Tips for Being Assertive*
- ☐ handout 6.5, *Refusing Assertively*
- ☐ handout 6.6, *Exercises: Refusing Assertively*
- ☐ handout 6.7, *Expressing Feelings Assertively*
- ☐ handout 6.8, *Exercises: Expressing Feeling Assertively*
- ☐ handout 6.9, *What Do You Know About Opiates?*
- ☐ handout 6.10, *Opiates*
- ☐ handout 6.11, *What Did You Learn?*

Preparation Needed

1. Read session 6 in its entirety to become familiar with it.

2. If you've provided binders or folders for participants, bring them along to distribute at the start of the session.

3. Photocopy all handouts and hole-punch if needed. Handouts appear in this book after each session outline; they can also be printed from the CD-ROM (if using a color printer, decorative elements will appear in color). During the session, distribute them one by one as prompted.

4. Arrange the room so that each participant can be included in the conversation.

5. If you created ground rules in session 1, post them for all participants to view.

6. Consider scenarios to use in the role-plays on pages 122 and 127. If you do not have a co-facilitator, think of conversations you can act out with participants.

How Important Is Communication?

This discussion helps participants think about the role communication plays in their daily lives. They will see how not communicating can easily lead to misunderstanding and conflict. In addition, they will discover that being judgmental when communicating can have an adverse impact.

Ask:

Going back to the canoe theme, how important is communication on a canoe journey? If you don't communicate well, what problems might occur?

Possible responses might include:

- People will have misunderstandings
- People won't get along
- People will argue
- People won't work in a coordinated effort
- People will be in danger

After the participants have come up with a list, review the possible answers listed above and suggest any important ones they might have missed.

Explain:

One traditional Native belief that applies to communication says:

"Everyone and everything was created with a specific purpose to fulfill; no one should have the power to interfere or to impose on others the best path to follow. What is required is that we seek our place in the universe and everything else will follow in good time."

TRADITIONAL

NATIVE BELIEF

Ask:

How does this teaching apply to communication?

Allow plenty of time for responses and make suggestions if no responses are given. Whatever points are made here, refer back to them throughout the session.

Two Ways of Communicating

Explain:

Communication is more than what we say. We communicate through our words, tone, silences, and physical stances. The best communication isn't about having the best advice or the biggest vocabulary; it is about letting the person we're talking with feel heard, understood, and important.

There are two ways of communicating: (1) nonverbally and (2) verbally.

Nonverbal Communication: Role-Play

> ▶ **Facilitator Tip**
> Two facilitators can pair up, or one facilitator can pick a participant to demonstrate specific nonverbal behaviors. Or participants can pair off and do this role-play themselves.

Explain:

Nonverbal communication is our body language and facial expressions. Let's role-play some nonverbal behavior.

Suggestions:

- A person standing and thinking (could be looking up, crossing arms and touching chin, looking puzzled, scratching head)
- A person looking bored (yawning, looking at watch, drumming fingers on a desk, sighing, looking sleepy)
- A person looking angry (frown, pout, furrowed brow, gritting teeth, breathing hard, pounding fist on the table)

After each role-play, ask:

What is this person communicating to you?

Verbal Communication

Explain using your own words:

We learn a great deal about individuals by observing their nonverbal behavior, but we also rely on verbal communication to express feelings, thoughts, and needs. We use verbal communication to:

- **listen to others**
- **explain our views**
- **give instructions**

There are two parts to verbal communication: (1) listening and (2) speaking.

EFFECTIVE LISTENING

Explain using your own words:

Effective listening takes practice and effort. We don't often think that it takes much effort because we are listening all the time. But think about it. If a person is not a good listener, what is he or she like? Is he or she a likeable individual?

Allow for responses.

Effective listening is an essential skill for making and keeping relationships. If you are a good listener, you'll notice that others are drawn to you. People who don't listen are boring. They don't seem interested in anyone but themselves.

Listening is a commitment to understanding how other people feel and how they see their world. Listening is a compliment because it says to the other person, "I care about what's happening to you. Your life and your experience are important."

Ask:

Going back to the canoe journey—why would it be important to be a good listener on the canoe journey?

Allow for responses.

Ask:

To be an effective listener, what skills do you need?

List the responses on the board.

Give each participant a copy of handout 6.1, "Tips for Effective Listening."

HANDOUT 6.1

121

**Listening Skills
Role-Play**

Explain:

**Now I would like to role-model good and bad listening skills.
First the bad.**

The two facilitators, or two participants, role-play bad listening skills. One player improvises to tell a story about the weekend, or important plans coming up, while the other player models bad listening behavior.

> ▶ **Facilitator Tip**
> A bad listener might read or watch TV while listening, act bored, interrupt, look at his/her watch, and act distracted.

Ask:

What kind of listener was this listener? What made this listener a bad listener?

Allow for responses.

Now let the same people perform the good listener role-play.

> ▶ **Facilitator Tip**
> A good listener will stop what he or she is doing, will look at the person who is talking, will nod his or her head saying "Uh-huh," "I understand," or "I see what you mean," will not interrupt, and will act interested.

Ask:

What made this listener a good listener?

Allow for responses.

Explain:

There are many cultural differences in being a good listener.

Ask:

Can you think of different ways that people from various cultures might listen?

Responses might include:

- may have limited eye contact
- may look away (either down or in the air)
- may stand very close
- may not give any indication that they are listening (long silences, no verbal responses, no head nods)

After the participants have come up with a list, review the possible answers listed above and suggest any they might have missed.

Learning to Communicate Assertively

Most people use predominantly one style of communication to get what they want or when they are in conflict, often to the detriment of their relationships. This material exposes participants to the various styles of communication and teaches them to use the healthiest and most effective style of communication: assertiveness.

Verbal Communication Styles: Aggressive, Passive, Assertive

HANDOUT 6.2

Explain using your own words:

Now, let's talk about effective verbal communication. There are basically three styles of verbal communication.

Give each participant a copy of handout 6.2, "Three Ways to Express Feelings."

Ask:

When someone communicates aggressively, what is that like?

Refer to the handout for some possible responses.

Ask:

When someone communicates passively, what is that like?

Refer to the handout for some possible responses.

Duplicating this page is illegal. Do not copy without publisher's written permission.

123

Ask:

When someone communicates assertively, what does this look like?

Refer to the handout for some possible responses.

Explain:

There are many cultural differences in expressing feelings.

Ask:

How do you think people from various cultures might express feelings?

Allow for responses and make suggestions if no responses are given. Responses might include:

- internalizing their feelings and, as a result, showing very little emotion to others.

- being very outspoken regarding their feelings and, as a result, showing lots of emotions.

Assertive Behavior

Explain using your own words:

Handout 6.2, under the category "Assertively," refers to making "I" statements.

Ask:

What are "I" statements?

Allow for responses.

Explain using your own words:

When we make "I" statements, we take responsibility for our own feelings and do not blame the other person. Instead of saying, "You make me so angry," we can choose to say, "I am upset."

There is one situation where communication can be very difficult: When we are having a conflict with someone. Let's look at a handout that gives you some tips about resolving conflict.

HANDOUT 6.3

HANDOUT 6.4

Give each participant a copy of handout 6.3, "Steps to Resolve Conflict."

Explain using your own words:

Assertiveness is effective because it allows you to have your needs met without hurting anyone else, it can help you resolve conflict, and it helps you remain calm under pressure. When you take these steps, you feel better and you will have done your best to maintain the relationship with the person that you had the conflict with.

Now let's look at some tips that will help you to be assertive.

Give each participant a copy of handout 6.4, "Tips for Being Assertive."

> ▶ **Facilitator Tip**
> Have participants take turns reading the tips aloud. Generate a discussion about each tip after it is read aloud.

Ask:

So now that we know what assertiveness is like, why do you think that it might be a useful skill to learn?

Allow for responses and make suggestions if no responses are given. Responses might include:

- creates a sense of personal satisfaction
- helps you get what you want
- increases your sense of being in control
- increases your sense of being honest
- increases respect and admiration from other people

Ask:

How many times have friends asked you to do something you didn't want to do, but you said yes just because you didn't want them to be angry with you?

Allow for responses.

HANDOUT 6.5

Explain using your own words:

Some people are brought up learning to be assertive, so it is a skill that they can use easily. But for the majority of us, assertiveness is something that we have to practice in order to do it well.

Now we want to look at some steps for making refusals—that is, saying no.

Give each participant a copy of handout 6.5, "Refusing Assertively."

Refusing Assertively

> ▶ **Facilitator Tip**
> Reinforce the following bulleted list by writing it on the board or flip chart.

Explain using your own words:

According to the handout, there are steps we can take to make a refusal assertively.

- **Stop and think about what you want**
- **Make the decision that is best for you**
- **Communicate your decision by first stating your position**
- **Explain your reason**
- **Express understanding OR**
- **Offer some alternative things to do**

Ask:

How might assertive behavior differ among cultures?

Allow for responses and make suggestions if no responses are given. Responses might include:

- Some cultures may be more vocal than others.
- Some cultures may use different body language, such as standing very close when talking.

Explain using your own words:

Remember: Taking the steps to be assertive allows you to take a firm stand and to express your opinions, feelings, and needs without hurting anybody's feelings.

Role-Play of Assertive Refusal

EXAMPLE 1

Explain:

Now we will role-model how to refuse someone assertively.

> ▶ **Facilitator Tip**
> If you are the only facilitator, ask a participant to read the co-facilitator's response.

Read the following script:

Facilitator: **"Hey, how about we skip work today and go shopping?"**

Co-facilitator: **"No, I can't do that because I need the money that I make from this job. I know how you feel, though, because sometimes I feel like taking time off work. Why don't we go shopping on one of our days off?"**

Ask:

Did you notice how she used the steps?

Explain:

1. **She first thought about what would be best for her.**

2. **She made a decision that was best for her.**

3. **She stated her position: "No, I can't."**

4. **She explained her reason: "I can't because I need the money that I make from this job."**

5. **She expressed understanding: "I know how you feel, though, sometimes I feel like taking time off work."**

6. **She offered an alternative: "Why don't we go shopping on one of our days off?"**

EXAMPLE 2

Explain:

Let's do another role-play.

If necessary, invite another participant to role-play.

Read the following script:

Facilitator: **"Hey, I heard that there is going to be a party this weekend at Steve's house. Do you want to go?"**

Co-facilitator: **"No, I can't go to his parties because I don't drink, and he always has drinking at his parties. Why don't we go to a movie instead?"**

Ask:

Did you notice how the steps were used in this situation?

Go over the steps according to handout 6.5.

Refusal of Harmful Behavior

Explain using your own words:

When practicing refusals of harmful behavior, it is not appropriate to make understanding statements. For example, you would not want to say, "I'm sorry I can't use cocaine with you but I hope you have luck getting someone else to snort it with you."

In this case it is most important to focus on the refusal and the reason.

A Right to Say *No*

Remember that you have a right to say no whenever you want to, but in some situations it isn't wise. For example, you are driving down the street and a police officer asks you to pull over. You have the right to say no—to keep driving—but you will have to accept the consequences that go along with saying no.

The point of saying "no" is to keep from being taken advantage of or to avoid doing something harmful. It is not to keep from engaging in daily responsibilities.

Ask:

So on a canoe journey, when might we have to practice our refusal skills?

Allow for responses.

Ask:

Now can you think of some examples of real-life situations where you might have to make assertive refusals?

Write the responses on the board. Once the list has been generated, pair off the participants and assign a situation from the list to each pair so they can do their own role-plays.

Explain:

That was a good exercise. Let's keep going, and this time we'll use a handout called "Assertive Refusal Exercises" for role-playing ideas.

Distribute handout 6.6 and allow time for more role-playing.

HANDOUT 6.6

Expressing Feelings

Explain:

Now let's look at how to express feelings assertively.

HANDOUT 6.7

Give each participant a copy of handout 6.7, "Expressing Feelings Assertively."

Explain using your own words:

There are three components to expressing feelings assertively:

- **Your perspective of the situation—"I think . . ."**
- **Your feelings about the situation—"I feel . . ."**
- **Your wants regarding the situation—"I want . . ."**

Ask:

How might people of other cultures express their feelings?

Allow for responses and make suggestions if no responses are given. Responses might include:

- Some cultures may express their feelings through actions such as hugging others.
- Some cultures may express their feelings by crying openly in front of others.

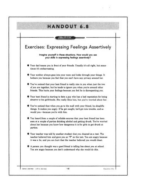

HANDOUT 6.8

Explain:

Now let's role-play expressing our feelings assertively.

Distribute handout 6.8, "Exercises: Expressing Feelings Assertively," and have participants continue role-playing.

Ask:

Getting back to the canoe, how might being able to express feelings assertively help us on our journey?

Allow for responses.

Ask:

How can being able to express our feelings assertively help us with our life's journey?

> Facilitator Tip
> Write down responses to the life journey question on the board. Have participants role-play situations with a partner.

Explain:

As I read the next traditional Native belief, think about how it applies to assertiveness.

TRADITIONAL
NATIVE BELIEF

"In order to be well, people must abide by beliefs about the balance between man and nature and about the importance of maintaining balance and harmony in our lives."

Ask:

How does this belief relate to being assertive?

Allow for responses and make suggestions if no responses are given.

Expressing Positive Feelings

Explain using your own words:

Expressing positive feelings and giving compliments are important skills in building healthy relationships. Complimenting people at school or work is an excellent way to demonstrate good social skills. It is important to have a good sense of what is appropriate in different situations. For example, it is not appropriate for people at work to make statements such as "Good job on that project. I love you!"

Opiates

In this discussion, participants become aware of the different kinds of opiates and gain an understanding of how they can interfere with the life journey.

Explain using your own words:

The next drug that we will be addressing is opiates. Before we look at the handout, let's see how much you already know about opiates.

Distribute handout 6.9, "What Do You Know About Opiates?" and let participants fill it out.

HANDOUT 6.9

Review the handout aloud, asking the group for answers. See if anyone knew all of them. (Brief answers are shown below; fuller answers are on handout 6.10.)

Brief Answer Key:
Handout 6.9, What Do You Know About Opiates?

1. What are opiates?

   Answer: Also called narcotics, they are pain relievers with a strong potential for abuse.

2. Are opiates legal or illegal?

   Answer: Some, like heroin, are illegal street drugs; others are prescribed for medical use.

3. Why are opiates so addictive?

   Answer: The brain cells become used to the substance and trigger withdrawal symptoms if they are deprived of it.

4. What are some common opiates?

   Answer: Heroin, and also prescription drugs such as codeine, methadone, morphine, and oxycodone.

5. What are the risks of taking opiates?

   Answer: Addiction, extreme weight loss and malnutrition, tremors, loss of judgment and self-control, severe medical problems.

6. What are some slang terms for opiates?

   Answer: Heroin—horse, junk, and smack; codeine—school boy; methadone—dollie; many others.

7. What happens when someone suddenly stops taking opiates?

   Answer: Withdrawal symptoms include chills and sweats, nausea and cramps, panic, insomnia, possible convulsions, or coma.

8. What is OxyContin?

   Answer: The brand name of oxycodone, a prescription painkiller with a high potential for abuse.

HANDOUT 6.10

Say:

Now let's look at another handout for more detailed answers.

Give each participant a copy of handout 6.10, "Opiates." Briefly review its contents.

Ask:

Would we want to take opiates on a canoe journey?

Allow for responses.

Say:

So that leads to the question that each of us should ask ourselves, "Do I want opiates to be a part of my life's journey?"

Conclusion

HANDOUT 6.11

Here participants summarize what has been learned throughout this session using the Medicine Wheel.

Give each participant a copy of handout 6.11, "What Did You Learn?"

Draw a Medicine Wheel on the board.

Ask:

Using the Medicine Wheel's four dimensions, what could we say that we have learned in this session?

Allow for responses. Suggest some of the following if the participants can't come up with their own. Possible answers might include:

Mental

- I've learned skills for effective communication.
- I've learned the effects of opiates on the brain.

Spiritual

- By communicating effectively, I can be content with myself.
- Confidence comes from taking a firm stand.

Physical

- By communicating aggressively, I can harm my body.
- I can actually relieve stress by communicating effectively and assertively.

Emotional

- Strength can be derived in difficult situations by communicating directly and effectively.
- I will feel more confidence and have a strong sense of well-being when I am able to say what I think and feel.

Ask each participant to share an item or two from the handout. Ask questions to spark discussion.

> ▶ **Facilitator Tip**
> Participants should be given time to complete the handout during the session. Do not allow participants to take the assignments home.

Tips for Effective Listening

Stop working.

Stop watching TV.

Stop reading.

Look at the person.

Keep a good distance between you and the speaker.

Don't turn away from the speaker.

Sit up straight.

Nod your head and make statements such as "Uh-huh," "I understand," and "I see what you mean" to show the speaker you truly understand what he/she is saying.

If you don't understand, let the person know that. Don't fake listening!

Repeat back phrases to clarify what the person is saying.

Ask questions to show that you are interested in what the person is saying.

Don't interrupt the speaker.

Three Ways to Express Feelings

Aggressively

A person expressing feelings aggressively:

- uses a loud voice, sometimes yelling
- uses abusive, disrespectful language
- dominates the conversation or interrupts
- is confrontive and tries to be intimidating
- can become physically threatening or abusive

Passively

A person expressing feelings passively:

- uses a quiet voice, says very little, or does not speak at all
- makes no eye contact; may look down
- makes indirect comments, hoping the other person will get the hint
- may bottle up feelings without expressing them at all
- avoids conflict as much as possible; does not confront directly
- is wishy-washy and takes no firm stand
- does not get his/her needs met

Assertively

A person expressing feelings assertively:

- speaks in a firm tone; stays fairly calm; makes eye contact
- makes "I" statements; gives reasons for feelings
- stands up for him/herself
- listens to what the other person is saying
- does not try to force another person to change, but states ideas for how to change the situation

Steps to Resolve Conflict

Control emotions. Use relaxation techniques. Take yourself out of the situation.

Express your feelings assertively.

Identify the reason for the conflict. Who is responsible? If needed, take time away from the person to think about the conflict and plan a strategy to resolve.

Ask the person: "Do you have time to talk?"

Tell the person how you are feeling, for example, "I am feeling upset right now."

Tell the person why you are feeling that way, for example, "You haven't paid your share of the rent for the last two months."

Listen. Listen. Listen. Allow the person to respond.

Discuss alternatives. Together, think of alternatives for resolving the conflict.

Discuss calmly. Continue to talk about the issue in a calm manner.

If the conflict seems to escalate and you find that you are getting angry, tell the person that you need to leave and you would like to talk about it later.

Tips for Being Assertive

Eye contact: Being direct involves some eye contact, but do not stare at people 100 percent of the time.

Body posture: Try to face the person. Stand or sit up tall.

Distance/physical contact: If you smell or feel the other person's breath, you are probably too close. Keep a comfortable distance.

Gestures: Use hand gestures to add to what you are saying.

Facial expressions: Your face should match your emotion and what you are saying. A pleasant face is best when you are happy. A serious face is best when you are upset.

Voice tone, inflection, and volume: In order to be heard you have to pay attention to the tone of your voice (happy, whiny, upset), the inflection of your voice (what words you stress), and the volume of your voice (from a whisper to a yell).

Fluency: It is important to get your words out. If a person stammers or rambles on, the listener will get bored.

Timing: If you have to express negative feelings or make a request of someone, do it as soon as there is a time for both parties to resolve their issues alone.

Listening: If you are making statements that express your feelings, you need to give the other person a chance to respond.

Content: What a person says is one of the most important parts of the assertive message.

Refusing Assertively

Example: A friend asks you to spend the night on a school night.

Stop and think about what you want.
Think: "Do I really want to spend the night?"

Make the decision that is best for you.
Think: "No, I don't think I want to spend the night tonight. It's a school night and I have homework."

Communicate your decision assertively by first stating your position.
State: "No, that is not a good idea for me."

Explain your reason.
Explain: "It's a school night and I have homework to do."

Express understanding.
Express: "I know how you are feeling. I get bored on school nights, too."

    or

Offer alternatives.
Suggest: "I think I can make plans to spend the night over the weekend. How does that sound?"

Exercises: Refusing Assertively

**Imagine yourself in these situations.
How would you use your assertive refusal skills?**

❶ A friend comes over to your house late at night and knocks on your window. She says she wants you to go walking around with her. You don't want to go but you don't want to hurt her feelings. How would you refuse her plan, using the steps for refusing assertively?

❷ A friend wants you to help him cheat on a test. You don't want to cheat, but you don't want to hurt your friend's feelings.

❸ Your uncle wants you to drive with him to the store, but he has been drinking. You don't want to offend him, but you also don't want to get in the car with him.

❹ Your best friend wants you to go with him to a party where there will be drinking. You don't want to go, but you don't want to hurt his feelings.

❺ Your boyfriend wants you to spend the night with him. You don't want to, but you don't want to make him mad.

❻ Your friend wants you to play a practical joke on a teacher. You don't want to because you will get into trouble, but you don't want to be accused of being a loser.

❼ Your friend wants you to go into a store and steal some candy for him. You don't want to get into trouble, but you don't want to make your friend unhappy.

❽ Your grandma asks you to come to her house to do some chores for her. You don't want to, but you don't want to hurt her feelings. (This is a trick question! We never refuse a grandma's request.)

Expressing Feelings Assertively

There are three components to expressing feelings assertively:

- Your perspective of the situation, "I think . . ."
- Your feelings about the situation, "I feel . . ."
- Your wants regarding the situation, "I want . . ."

Example: Your best friend said that she would pick you up at 7:00 tonight. It is now 9:00 and she still has not appeared.

- "I think . . ."

   She said that she would pick me up at 7:00 and I am still waiting for her two hours later.

- "I feel . . ."

   I feel angry and hurt because I feel that she is inconsiderate and obviously doesn't care about how I feel.

- "I want . . ."

   When I see her I am going to tell her that I want her to consider my feelings and at least call me if she is going to be late.

Exercises: Expressing Feelings Assertively

Imagine yourself in these situations. How would you use your skills in expressing feelings assertively?

❶ Your dad teases you in front of your friends. Usually it's all right, but sometimes it's embarrassing.

❷ Your mother always goes into your room and looks through your things. It bothers you because you feel that you can't have any privacy around her.

❸ You've noticed that your best friend is really nice to you when just the two of you are together, but he tends to ignore you when you're around other friends. This hurts your feelings because you feel he is disrespecting you.

❹ Your best friend is starting to date a guy who has a bad reputation for being abusive to his girlfriends. She really likes him, but you're worried about her.

❺ You've noticed that when you go to the mall with your friend, he shoplifts things. It makes you angry. If he got caught, he'd get into trouble, and so would you—because you're with him.

❻ You heard from a couple of reliable sources that your best friend has been seen at a couple of parties drinking alcohol and getting drunk. You're worried about her because you know how dangerous it is for girls to get drunk at parties.

❼ Your teacher was told by another student that you cheated on a test. The teacher believed him and gave you an "F" on the test. You are angry because it was a lie, and you are hurt that the teacher believed you would cheat.

❽ A person you thought was a good friend is telling lies about you at school. You are angry because you don't understand why she would do this.

What Do You Know About Opiates?

❶ What are opiates?

❷ Are opiates legal or illegal?

❸ Why are opiates so addictive?

❹ What are some common opiates?

❺ What are the dangers of long-term opiate use?

❻ What are some slang terms for opiates?

❼ What happens when someone suddenly stops taking opiates?

❽ What is OxyContin?

Opiates

Often called narcotics, these highly addictive drugs relieve pain and can also trigger a high if abused. Some opiates are illegal "street drugs" such as heroin; others are legal prescription drugs such as codeine, morphine, methadone, Dilaudid, and Demerol. Another of these, oxycodone, has had high abuse rates in recent years. Sold under trade names such as OxyContin, Percocet, and Percodan, it is a time-release tablet whose effects should be gradual. But abusers seeking a high may chew the tablets or crush them into a powder that can be snorted or dissolved for injection.

Opiates work by depressing the central nervous system, and long-term use actually changes brain function. The cells get so used to the opiate that they can't work without it! If an addicted user suddenly stops, the dependent nerve cells become overactive and prompt withdrawal symptoms ranging from chills, cramps, and nausea to panic and convulsions. Eventually, though, the brain can recover and work normally again.

Slang terms for some opiates:

Codeine: School Boy • Dilaudid: Little D • Methadone: Dollie
Morphine: M; Miss Emma • Opium: Dover's Powder

Heroin, an illegal opiate, can be smoked, snorted, or injected into the veins ("IV"), muscle, or just under the skin ("skin-popping"). It activates the brain regions that are responsible for both the pleasurable feeling of "reward" and for physical addiction. Heroin addiction is marked by continuous cravings. The exact strength of a given dose is always uncertain: another danger factor for users.

Slang terms: *Horse, junk, Mexican Brown, skag, hard stuff, smack*

Short-term effects of heroin:

- euphoria
- reduced hunger and sex drive
- shallow breathing; drowsiness and heavy limbs
- cramps, constipation, nausea, vomiting
- raw, red nostrils from snorting
- excessive itching and scratching

CONTINUED ON NEXT PAGE

Long-term effects of heroin:

- malnutrition; extreme loss of appetite and weight
- needle tracks or punctures; scars along veins
- bruises from "skin popping"
- poor vision and concentration
- tremors; irritability; apathy
- loss of judgment and self-control
- tolerance and addiction

Medical risks of heroin use:

- heart valve infection and cardiac disease; congested lungs and pneumonia
- skin abscesses; vein inflammation; higher risk of contracting HIV (for IV users)
- liver disease; serum hepatitis; tetanus; anemia
- ever-present risk that an unusually potent dose will lead to overdose, coma, death

Note: Cocaine and crack are opiates, but are discussed in handout 3.4, "Stimulants."

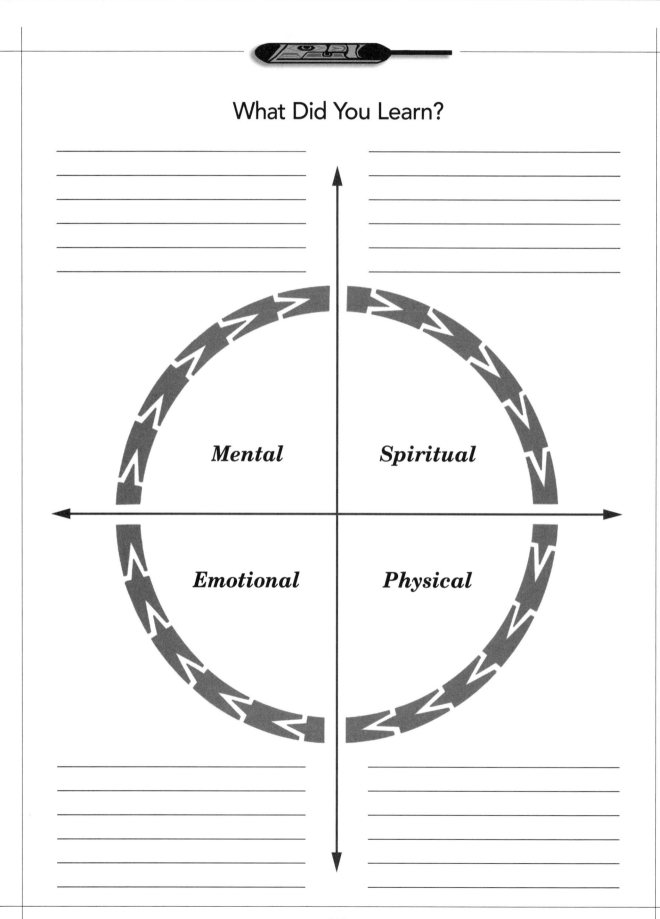

What Did You Learn?

Mental

Spiritual

Emotional

Physical

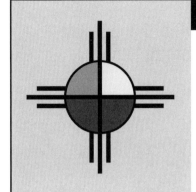

Moods

COPING WITH NEGATIVE EMOTIONS

Purpose of Session 7

In this session, participants learn that how they react to events is based more on their own perceptions than on the event itself. They learn to consciously take control of their emotions and discover positive steps to improve many life situations.

Learner Outcomes

By the end of this session, participants will be able to:

- identify various emotions
- describe negative and positive self-talk
- recognize signs of depression and suicide
- determine ways to cope with negative emotions

Materials Needed

- ☐ flip chart, white board, or chalk board
- ☐ markers or chalk
- ☐ peanut M&Ms or other treat (one for each participant)—have non-nut options for those with allergies
- ☐ handout 7.1, *ABC Analysis of Emotional Reactions*
- ☐ handout 7.2, *Symptoms of Adolescent Depression*
- ☐ handout 7.3, *Suicide Danger Signs*
- ☐ handout 7.4, *Inhalants*
- ☐ handout 7.5, *Methamphetamine*

MATERIALS NEEDED CONTINUED ON NEXT PAGE

☐ handout 7.6, *Inhalants Worksheet* (one copy only)

☐ handout 7.7, *Methamphetamine Worksheet* (one copy only)

☐ handout 7.8, *What Did You Learn?*

Preparation Needed

1. Read session 7 in its entirety to become familiar with it.

2. If you've provided binders or folders for participants, bring them along to distribute at the start of the session.

3. Photocopy all handouts and hole-punch if needed. Handouts appear in this book after each session outline; they can also be printed from the CD-ROM (if using a color printer, decorative elements will appear in color). During the session, distribute them one by one as prompted.

4. Bring enough peanut M&Ms for each participant to have one. Bring non-nut options for those with allergies.

5. Arrange the room so that each participant can be included in the conversation.

6. If you created ground rules in session 1, post them for all participants to view.

Emotional Balance: On the Canoe Journey

The purpose here is to introduce participants to the concept that life requires some degree of emotional balance if we are to be at our best.

Ask:

Going back to the canoe journey, how important do you think it is to have your emotions in control on a canoe journey?

Allow for responses. Write them on the flip chart or board. Responses might include the following:

- If people get depressed, they won't be very helpful.

- Arguments and fights might break out.

- A person's fear of water might interfere with being on the canoe.

- Negative emotions may interfere with progress on the journey.

Read the following:

One traditional Native belief that applies to what we will be learning in this session is:

TRADITIONAL

NATIVE BELIEF

"The seen and the unseen are equally important. The physical world is real, and the spiritual world is real. They are two aspects of one reality, yet there are separate laws that govern each of them. A balanced life is one that honors both worlds."

Ask:

Can you think of how this belief may apply to this session on emotions?

Allow for responses. Responses might include the following:

- A spiritual life will help us deal with our emotions.

- Emotions impact how we see the world.

Identifying Emotions

In this section, participants identify a wide range of feelings, consider how it feels to experience these emotions, and become more aware of how our feelings impact our behavior.

Explain using your own words:

We all have a number of emotions. Let's try to name as many as we can.

Write the responses on the board. Participants typically assume this is an easy task, but soon find it harder than they think. The list should include at least the five basic emotions: anger, sadness, gladness, shame, and fear.

Explain using your own words:

There are many ways that people act and feel with different emotions.

Ask:

How do you behave when you are happy?

Write responses on the board.

Ask:

Where do you feel it in your body?

Write responses on the board.

Ask:

How do you behave when you are angry?

Write responses on the board.

Ask:

Where do you feel it in your body?

Write responses on the board.

Ask:

How do you behave when you are sad?

Write responses on the board.

Ask:

Where do you feel it in your body?

Write responses on the board.

Explain using your own words:

The point is that we behave in different ways depending on the emotion. We also feel different depending on the emotion we are feeling, and we actually have distinct bodily reactions (or physiological reactions) depending on the emotion we are feeling.

All emotions are okay, but negative behaviors as a result of those feelings are not okay.

What Causes Emotional Reactions?

This section puts emotional reactions into perspective. Participants see that they often react out of their own conditioning, and they will learn that they have choices regarding how they express their emotions.

Explain using your own words:

Emotions come and go, but what causes that to happen?

Allow for responses.

Say:

Emotions are reactions to events that happen in the outside environment: for example, a death in the family, a relationship breakup, the birth of a child, a slap in the face.

Or . . . emotions can be reactions to events that occur inside of us. In other words, a person's own thoughts, behaviors, and physical reactions can cause an emotional response.

AUTOMATIC REACTIONS

Explain using your own words:

Some events seem to prompt emotions automatically. We seem to have a reaction without having had thoughts about the event. For example: When we see a car accident occur,

Duplicating this page is illegal. Do not copy without publisher's written permission.

151

we are "automatically" shocked and horrified. Or, when we see a beautiful sunset, we automatically feel joy.

LEARNED REACTIONS

These are not actually automatic reactions; they are learned. For example, if a baby sees a car accident occur, she is not shocked and horrified. She might be startled by the noise but little else.

That same baby may see a beautiful sunset and not feel joy automatically. As the child matures, she learns the significance of certain events and learns to respond in a particular way.

"ABC" Analysis of Emotional Reactions

HANDOUT 7.1

Explain using your own words:

Most people think that an event or a situation causes an emotional reaction. But this is not how an emotional reaction occurs.

Give each participant a copy of handout 7.1, "ABC Analysis of Emotional Reactions."

Explain using your own words:

Sometimes it seems our feelings are triggered directly by what happens around us. The handout shows how an "activating event" seems to lead directly to our reaction.

ACTIVATING EVENT ⟶ EMOTIONAL REACTION

But that's not quite true. Most emotions are the product of a person's interpretation of an event—that is, the person's belief about it. The event occurs, and then the person interprets it, or has a belief about it, which prompts the emotional reaction.

In this analysis, "A" stands for the activating event. "B" stands for our belief about it—our interpretation of it. And "C" stands for the consequence: the feeling we have.

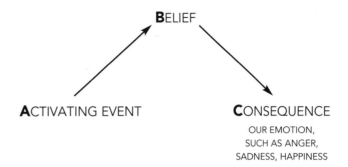

Explain using your own words:

So it's what we believe, or how we interpret the event, that causes the emotion to occur.

"ABC" Example

Read the following example.

ACTIVATING EVENT:

Someone offers you alcohol at a party.

BELIEF OR INTERPRETATION:

You might interpret this event in many ways, depending on your past experience with alcohol. You may think,

- **I tried alcohol before and . . .**
- **It makes me feel too weird.**
- **It makes me obnoxious, and I act stupid.**
- **It did nothing for me.**
- **It made me feel relaxed, and I enjoyed the buzz.**

Or you may think,

- **I don't believe in drinking alcohol.**

You will make the decision to drink or not to drink based on what you believe.

CONSEQUENCE:

Depending on your belief or interpretation, you may feel:

- **Annoyance**
- **Indifference: it's no big deal; you shrug it off**
- **Anger**
- **Anticipation**

Ask participants to generate more examples and use the ABC analysis to evaluate them.

Explain using your own words:

The main point is that we can choose to interpret events in many different ways. If we put a positive interpretation on events that occur in our lives, we will tend to be happier and more content in our daily lives.

Ask:

If we put a negative interpretation on events that occur in our lives, how would we tend to feel?

Allow for responses, which may include the following:

- angry
- sad
- resentful
- depressed

Anger

The purpose of this section is to get participants to see how anger, the emotion that can cause much harm, is okay to feel and that they can express it without being hurtful. They will see that anger, like other emotions, is subjective. Not everyone gets angry over the same events. Participants will learn the value of expressing anger positively and will recognize harmful expressions of anger.

Explain using your own words:

Anger is an important emotion to examine because it has the potential to create lots of problems.

Ask:

If you were a person who loses your temper often and acts out aggressively when you are angry, how long would you last on a canoe journey?

Allow for responses.

Explain using your own words:

Needless to say, losing one's temper could be disruptive on a canoe journey.

Ask:

How many times have you heard someone say, "You make me so angry"? Is it true that someone can make you angry?

Explain using your own words:

We learned from the ABC analysis that it is how we interpret events that causes a particular emotional reaction. The emotion that we experience is based on our past experiences.

Anger: An ABC Example

Read the following aloud:

A friend told me that she received flowers from her husband.

"That's great!" I told her.

"No, it isn't. I hate it when he does that!" she said.

"I don't understand. Most people like to get flowers from their loved ones."

"I know, but it means something different when he gives me flowers. It either means that he is trying to get something from me or that he is covering up for something he did. It really makes me feel angry when he gives me flowers and I hate it!"

Explain using your own words:

Let's apply the ABC analysis to this situation.

ACTIVATING EVENT:

Getting flowers from her husband.

BELIEF:

He is trying to get something from me, or he is covering up for something that he did.

CONSEQUENCE:

Anger, resentment, annoyance.

Ask:

Is there anything wrong with feeling anger?

Explain:

No, anger is a normal, natural emotional response to being hurt, frustrated, or feeling disrespected. There is nothing wrong with feeling anger, but it becomes problematic if we deal with it in unhealthy ways.

Unhealthy Anger Responses

Ask:

What are two unhealthy ways that many people deal with anger?

Two answers are

- **They stuff or repress their anger**
- **They act out by becoming violent**

Ask:

Why is stuffing or repressing our anger unhealthy?

Allow for responses.

Explain using your own words:

It is not healthy to hold anger in or to pretend that we are not feeling angry. Stuffing our anger is a problem because it means that we are denying our feelings. In some people, it can lead to depression. Some people keep thinking about what makes them angry and it builds up until they explode.

Ask:

Why is violence an unhealthy way to deal with our anger?

Allow for responses.

Explain using your own words:

Anger is an emotion, and violence is an inappropriate way to express the emotion. When we act out our anger aggressively, there is a risk of harming ourselves and others.

Appropriate Responses to Anger

Explain using your own words:

We need to learn to direct our anger in appropriate ways. The first way to learn to deal with anger is to recognize when we are feeling it.

Ask:

How do you feel when you are angry? Where do you feel it in your body?

Allow for responses, which might include the following:

- We feel tension in neck, chest, arms, legs, face, and stomach
- Our heart starts pounding
- We breathe faster
- Blood rushes to our face

Ask:

Let's say that you are in a situation where you find that you are angry. What should you do?

Explain using your own words:

There are many effective ways to deal with anger, and the following are just three of those ways:

COUNT TO TEN.

Many people dismiss this simple way to deal with anger. But it actually works because it distracts you from your anger. It is difficult for anyone to concentrate on two things at once. When you are thinking about something as simple as counting, you stop thinking about what is making you angry.

REASON WITH YOURSELF.

Talk yourself out of being upset: ask yourself questions to determine if your anger is worth an aggressive action. You might ask:

- Is the matter worthy of my continued attention?
- Am I justified in feeling the way I do?
- Do I have an effective response?

TAKE A TIME-OUT.

Leave the situation until you calm down.

Learn to direct your anger considerately to the appropriate person by using assertiveness skills. Assertive behavior can help stop aggressive behavior. You state how you feel and then express what you need.

- I feel angry because . . .
- I would like . . .

If you can't talk to the person you are angry with, talk to a friend or therapist about your anger.

Ask:

Can you think of other ways to deal with out-of-control anger?

Allow for responses.

Explain using your own words:

Knowing what we are feeling and thinking and having strategies to avoid out-of-control behavior can be very helpful in coping with anger and other strong feelings.

Self-Talk

Explain using your own words:

Another behavior that can lead to negative feelings involves what we say to ourselves. We all have a running dialogue that is almost constantly going on in our heads. So even as I am talking, there are thoughts going through your head.

You may be thinking any of these kinds of thoughts:

- **Gosh, this person is such an interesting, dynamic speaker!**
- **Gosh, this is so boring. I hope it's over soon.**
- **My stomach is growling. It must be getting close to lunchtime.**
- **My boyfriend said he would call me tonight. I hope he does.**

The point is that we have thoughts going through our mind all the time, even when we are listening to interesting speakers.

MIRROR SELF-TALK

Explain using your own words:

Looking in the mirror is an example of self-talk. Most of us look in a mirror many times a day.

Ask:

What do you say to yourself when you look in the mirror?

Allow for responses, then give the following examples:

- "I look good today!"
- "Oh no, I'm gaining weight. I look fat!"
- "Gosh, I sure look good in this outfit."
- "Boy, I'm having a bad hair day."

Explain using your own words:

So the next time you look into a mirror, pay attention to what you say to yourself. If the dialogue tends to be negative, reframe your thoughts so they are positive.

Ask:

Why would thinking more positively be beneficial?

Allow for responses, which might include the following:

- By thinking positively, I feel that anything is possible.
- By thinking positively, I feel so much better about myself.

MAKING MISTAKES

Explain using your own words:

Another example of self-talk is what we say to ourselves when we make a mistake. We can think many different thoughts, both positive and negative.

- **"Oh, I'm so stupid. I never do anything right."**

- **"Well, that was a mistake, but everybody makes mistakes, so that's okay. At least now I will know what I should do next time."**

The point is that thoughts, feelings, and actions are related, and we can make the decision to change our thoughts so that we can be more positive and feel better in our lives.

Depression

In this section participants learn what depression looks like, what causes it, and when it becomes dangerous. Participants will feel empowered knowing they can take steps to help themselves or others who are feeling depressed or suicidal.

Explain using your own words:

Now I would like to talk about a problem that affects a lot of young people: depression.

Ask:

What kinds of events bring out sadness or a depressed mood in us?

Allow for responses and write them on the board. You will need to refer to them again later in the session. Some responses might be:

- death
- a sad movie
- someone else's sadness
- a relationship breakup

**Depression
Symptoms**

Ask:

How do you know if someone is depressed? What is their behavior like?

Allow for responses.

HANDOUT 7.2

Explain using your own words:

Let's look at some of the typical symptoms of depression.

Give each participant a copy of handout 7.2, "Symptoms of Adolescent Depression."

Explain using your own words:

You're probably thinking, "Hey, I have some of those symptoms. I must be depressed." All of us get some of these symptoms sometimes, but that doesn't necessarily mean that we are depressed. To be diagnosed as having clinical depression, you must experience at least five of these symptoms for more than two weeks. If you find that you have five of these symptoms for more than two weeks, you should seek help: talk to a doctor, mental health professional, parents, a teacher, or a mentor.

**Suicide
Danger Signs**

Ask:

All of these symptoms are uncomfortable, but which of them can be life-threatening?

Allow for responses, which might include the following:

- thoughts of death and suicide

HANDOUT 7.3

Ask:

Sometimes when people feel sad, they may think that life is hopeless or not worth living. How would you know if a friend wanted to kill himself or herself?

Allow for responses.

Give each participant a copy of handout 7.3, "Suicide Danger Signs." Generate a discussion about the signs.

Duplicating this page is illegal. Do not copy without publisher's written permission.

161

What to Do?

Ask:

If you see a friend displaying any of these behaviors, what should you do?

Have the participants generate a list of things they would do and write them on the board. The list might include the following:

- Tell a teacher
- Tell a medical person
- Tell parents
- Call a crisis line

Explain using your own words:

Suicide is a permanent "solution" to a temporary problem, and there are a lot of things that can be done to solve the problems that are making the person feel hopeless.

Coping with Negative Emotions

In this section participants discuss the positive and negative ways people cope with negative emotions.

SELF-MEDICATING BEHAVIOR

Explain using your own words:

We have spent a good deal of time talking about negative emotions and how to identify them. Now let's talk about things that we can do to cope with negative feelings and emotions. One thing we might choose is called self-medicating behavior.

Ask:

Does anyone know what self-medicating means?

Allow for responses.

Explain using your own words:

Self-medicating means using drugs or alcohol as a way to cope with negative emotions we are feeling.

> **For example, we might:**
>
> - **drink alcohol to deal with the pain of our parents' divorce**

• **smoke pot to try to relieve loneliness**

• **get high to feel good and forget**

Ask:

Is this an effective way to deal with feelings? Can anyone think of why this might not be a good solution to our problems?

Allow for responses and create a list on the board. The list might include the following:

• doesn't offer a real solution; problems still exist

• stunts emotional maturation

• distracts from learning healthy, productive coping behaviors

• could lead to dependence on alcohol/drugs

• drugs/alcohol can make problems like depression worse

Explain using your own words:

Trying to avoid feelings by using alcohol or other drugs is tempting, but ultimately accepting and feeling the sadness (or any other negative emotion) is the only way to get through the experience.

Changing Our Actions

Explain using your own words:

We have talked about coping behaviors that might have consequences we don't want. Now let's talk about what we can do to change our actions in other ways to help cope with situations when we feel sad, angry, or anxious. Sometimes, there is something wrong with the situation. We can think about what we can do to change the situation.

Read the following:

One traditional Native belief that refers to the concept of change says:

TRADITIONAL NATIVE BELIEF

"Change is constant but occurs in cycles or patterns. Change is not accidental or random. Human beings must be active participants in the changes in their lives."

Ask:

What does this Native belief say about changing and coping?

Allow for responses, which might include the following:

- Since change is constant, I need to learn ways of coping with it.
- Watch for the patterns and cycles of change.

Explain using your own words:

One important strategy that we can use and have already talked about (in session 5) is to change our actions through problem-solving skills.

Ask:

Remember the steps to problem solving?

Read the following list as you write it on the board:

1. **Define the problem**

2. **Brainstorm solutions**

3. **Pick the solution you think is best**

4. **Make a plan to carry out the solution**

5. **Act on it**

6. **Review and revise it**

Explain using your own words:

Let's go back to some of the examples you came up with of situations that can make you feel depressed or sad and apply the problem-solving skills.

Refer to the list of situations that can trigger depression. They should still be on the board or flip chart. If not, choose a different example. The goal is to show how problem solving leads to a behavioral response that alters the situation and thus alters mood. When problem solving, assertiveness often comes into play. If applicable, point out when participants are using the assertiveness skills they learned in session 6.

KEEP LIFE IN BALANCE

Explain using your own words:

Remember the Native belief that we read earlier that said that in order to be well we must maintain balance and harmony in our lives? We can actually start feeling depressed or sad when our life gets out of balance. This happens if we have nothing to do or when we are too busy. Sometimes we can start feeling sad or depressed just because we aren't doing many fun activities or getting together with friends to do positive things.

PHYSICAL EXERCISE

Explain using your own words:

Exercise is one great way to change your mood so you feel better. When you exercise, you not only have something to do, but you also help your body stay healthy. Exercise also releases chemicals in the brain called endorphins, which are natural mood enhancers; that is, they make you feel happier.

Ask:

Exercise should be fun. What are some fun ways to exercise?

Write the responses on the board or flip chart.

Explain using your own words:

Following are some things to keep in mind about exercise:

- **It's best to do more than one type of exercise, so that if something gets in the way of your regular exercise (like it's raining too hard to hike) you can do something else easily.**

- **When you first start exercising it's sometimes not as fun as it will be later. Give it a little time, start slow, and don't expect to be perfect.**

- **Adding exercise to your lifestyle can be one of the best things you ever do because you will be strengthening your body as well as helping your mood.**

- **When necessary, you will be able to use exercise to cope, even in situations where you really can't fix the problem.**

Duplicating this page is illegal. Do not copy without publisher's written permission.

165

RELAXATION

Explain using your own words:

When we get upset or angry, so do our bodies. If we get upset or angry, our heart rate increases, our muscles tighten, and we may start to sweat, among other things. To deal with our emotions, we need to calm our bodies, and we can do this by using various relaxation techniques.

Relaxation techniques increase awareness of:

- **muscle tension and our ability to control that tension**
- **autonomic activity (involuntary functions like breathing, heart rate, blood flow)**
- **cognitive activity (what we're thinking)**

Deep breathing is just one relaxation technique that you can practice daily for about ten to fifteen minutes.

Do either the deep breathing or the mindfulness exercise in class.

DEEP BREATHING

Go through the following procedure as a group or just explain how to do it and skip to the mindfulness exercise.

Doing deep breathing is a great way to relieve stress.

- **Find a comfortable room with a comfortable chair. Sit and relax. Arms and legs should be uncrossed. Hands should rest on the stomach.**
- **Breathe in through your nose for a count of four, filling your lungs with air. Place your hands on chest or stomach area and note the expansion and contraction. This means that you are breathing deep breaths.**
- **Exhale the air slowly through your mouth for a count of six.**
- **Do this about ten times when you are trying to calm down.**

MINDFULNESS

Go through the following procedure as a group or, if you did the deep breathing exercise, just explain how to do the mindfulness exercise.

Another strategy that can be used to cope with negative feelings and thoughts is called mindfulness.

Mindfulness is experiencing and observing exactly what is happening in the moment. The idea is to focus the mind and awareness on the current moment's activity. Achieving such focus requires constantly controlling our attention. It is helpful because many times our minds are preoccupied with worries, so much so that we become tense and anxious. Mindfulness allows us to take a break from those worries.

Mindfulness: An M&M Candy Exercise

Now we're going to do an exercise to practice mindfulness. I'm going to give you one peanut M&M to eat. If you don't eat nuts, tell me. I have another option for you.

> ▶ **Facilitator Tip**
> First explain the exercise, then hand out the candy. Have a different treat available in case any participants are allergic to or don't like peanuts.

Continue, using your own words:

I would like you to eat the candy differently than you may be accustomed to. I want you to place it in your mouth and be mindful, be aware, of the experience of eating one M&M. When you place it in your mouth, be aware of the movement, and observe how it feels in your mouth, what it tastes like, and maybe even your emotional response to it. Now eat it very slowly, being aware of everything that is happening. You may even peel the crunchy layer off of the top and feel the crunchiness in your mouth. Feel the smoothness of the chocolate inside the shell. Observe how it tastes and feels in your mouth. Then, after you have eaten the chocolate, experience the sensations as you chew the peanut inside. And as you are doing all of this, breathe gently and deeply.

Duplicating this page is illegal. Do not copy without publisher's written permission.

167

Distribute the candy and be sure to tell everyone to wait until you tell them to put the candy in their mouth.

Explain:

Close your eyes, place the candy in your mouth, and eat it mindfully.

Give them some time, then ask:

So what is it like to eat an M&M mindfully?

Encourage several responses.

Ask:

When you were eating the M&M, how much attention were you able to spend thinking about other things?

Allow for responses.

Ask:

So can you see how using mindfulness can give you a little rest from your anxieties and worries?

> ▶ **Facilitator Tip**
> You can choose any type of food to do the mindfulness exercise. You can also choose to do any other activity that involves using one of the five senses.

Can't Change the Situation?

Ask:

What if you have a situation you can't change? How does this make you feel?

Allow for responses.

Explain using your own words:

This can often be the case when you lose or are losing someone because they have died or are dying, your parents divorce, you have to move, or if a friendship is ending.

ACCEPTANCE

Explain using your own words:

In these cases, sadness and grief arc natural, and it's impossible not to experience these feelings. It's hard to believe, but acknowledging and accepting feelings of sadness, pain, and grief, even though very difficult, is the only thing that will make you feel better in the long run.

You can't keep your parents from divorcing, but you can:

- **do things to improve your relationship with your parents and find ways to see each of them.**
- **understand that what's happening in your family is not your fault.**
- **understand that it has to do with the adult relationship and not with anything you did or didn't do.**

SOCIAL SUPPORT

Another thing you can do is to continue to keep in touch with your family, friends, and the adults in your community. Use your support people even if you don't always feel like it.

OTHER COPING STRATEGIES

Ask:

What are some other activities that can help you cope with sadness?

Allow for responses and be sure to include the following:

- talk to a friend
- read a book
- take a bubble bath

Say:

These are important to do even when you don't feel like it.

Duplicating this page is illegal. Do not copy without publisher's written permission.

169

**Expressing
Your Feelings**

Ask:

**What are some ways to help you express your feelings and
keep from becoming overwhelmed?**

Generate a list on the board or flip chart. Be sure to include
the following:

• writing in a journal about what's happening

• drawing or painting pictures about what's going on

INCREASE INVOLVEMENT

Explain:

**Increasing your involvement with family and community
helps provide support in stressful times. Enjoy pleasurable
activities with them. Putting some regular coping skills like
exercise or meditation into your routine can also help with
almost any problem that comes up in your life.**

**All of these strategies will help with depressive feelings and
grief, but they can also be useful in dealing with anger and
stress.**

**Inhalants and
Methamphetamine**

HANDOUT 7.4

Explain:

**What about using drugs to deal with depression, grief, anger,
and stress? They actually make those problems much worse.
We're going to talk about two groups of drugs that are often
easy to find: inhalants and methamphetamine. They may be
tempting for a quick high, but they can ruin your life—fast.**

**Now we'll look at some facts about that. Let's form two
groups for a relay race. One group will focus on inhalants,
and the other will focus on methamphetamine.**

Form two groups and, if needed,
ask them to sit together.

Pass out handout 7.4, "Inhalants,"
to the first group and handout 7.5,
"Methamphetamine," to the second
group.

HANDOUT 7.5

HANDOUT 7.6

HANDOUT 7.7

Then give the first group one copy of handout 7.6, and the second group one copy of handout 7.7. They will use these worksheets to answer your questions, one at a time.

Explain to all participants:

I will give each group one question at a time. The group will find the correct answer on their handout, write the answer down, and pass it to me. I'll tell them if the answer is right, and if it is, the group can go on to the next question. If it's wrong, the group tries again. The two groups will be working at the same time. The team that answers all the questions correctly in the fastest time will win the relay.

> **Facilitator Tip**
> See pages 172–173 for the questions you will ask and the answers to expect. You can either ask the questions out loud (one at a time), or write them down in advance on slips of paper and hand them in sequence to each group.

Conclusion

Give each participant a copy of handout 7.8, "What Did You Learn?"

Ask:

Using the Medicine Wheel's four dimensions, what could we say that we have learned in this session?

Give participants time to write down answers in each of the four categories: mental, spiritual, emotional, and physical. You may choose to draw the Medicine Wheel on the board and ask participants to offer some responses. If they can't come up with their own, offer a few examples, such as:

Mental

- I have learned about the relationship between thoughts, feelings, and actions.
- I have learned some common symptoms of someone who is suicidal.

These examples continue on page 174.

HANDOUT 7.8

Duplicating this page is illegal. Do not copy without publisher's written permission.

171

Facilitator Q and A: Inhalants	
QUESTIONS	**ANSWERS**
1. What is huffing?	Inhaling chemical substances to get high.
2. What is SSD?	Sudden sniffing death.
3. If someone I know is huffing and in a state of crisis, what should I do?	Get help; call Emergency Medical Services. Make sure the person can breathe and does not inhale vomit.
4. Out of ten first-time users, how many will not survive the experience?	One person in ten dies using inhalants for the first time.
5. Inhalant abusers use what common products to huff?	Spray paint, paint thinner, felt-tip markers, adhesives, fabric protectors, acetone products, carburetor cleaner, gasoline, and propane gas.
6. Name three organs that can be damaged by inhalants.	Brain, heart, and lungs.
7. If the inhalant user is not breathing, what should you do?	Administer CPR (cardiopulmonary resuscitation).
8. Can nosebleeds be an early symptom of huffing?	Yes.
9. Killing brain cells can result in what conditions?	Personality changes, memory and learning problems, loss of coordination, slurred speech, and tremors.
10. How long does the inhalant high last?	15 to 45 minutes.

Facilitator Q and A: Methamphetamine	
QUESTIONS	**ANSWERS**
1. What happens to a meth user after the initial energy rush?	After the high comes a devastating crash that often makes the user desperate for the high again.
2. Name four of meth's withdrawal symptoms.	For example: depression, anxiety, fatigue, cravings, paranoia, and aggression.
3. What is "tolerance" for methamphetamine?	When users build tolerance, they need more of the drug to get the same effect.
4. What are five slang terms for methamphetamine?	Speed, tweak, uppers, chalk, zip, and amp. (For crystal meth: crystal, ice, crank, and glass.)
5. What is a common hallucination for meth users?	The sensation of insects crawling over the skin.
6. Name four ways meth can be taken.	It can be swallowed, snorted, injected, or smoked.
7. What are some household products used to make meth?	For example: battery acid, drain cleaner, and antifreeze.
8. What group of drugs does meth belong to?	Stimulants.
9. Name four of meth's long-term effects on the user.	For example: psychotic behavior and paranoia, hallucinations, homicidal and suicidal thoughts, rage, and violence.
10. What kinds of brain damage can result from long-term meth use?	Loss of memory and ability to process information and make decisions. Brain cell loss can also result in body-movement disorders such as involuntary muscle spasms and twitches.

- I have learned how to cope with negative thoughts.
- I now know how to stay in control of myself.

Spiritual

- I know some of the symptoms of depression.
- I have ideas on helping someone who is suicidal.
- By remaining spiritual, I can more easily control my thoughts and feelings.
- Confidence comes from making a firm stand.

Physical

- I have learned how depression affects people physically.
- I have learned how to change my mood through exercise, relaxation, and meditation.
- I have learned how to accept my emotions.

Emotional

- I have learned how to control my thoughts, feelings, and actions.
- I have learned that I can interpret situations in life in many different ways.
- I have learned how to interpret events in a more positive light and how this can help with a depressed mood.

Allow the participants time to complete the handout and discuss some of their ideas.

> ▶ **Facilitator Tip**
> Participants should be given time to complete the handout during the session. Do not allow participants to take the assignments home.

"ABC" Analysis of Emotional Reactions

When something happens to us, it might seem like that event triggers our emotional reaction.

ACTIVATING EVENT ⟶ **EMOTIONAL REACTION**

But this is not really how an emotional reaction occurs!

Most feelings are prompted by our interpretation of an event—what we believe or think about it. We have "A," an activating event, followed by "B," our belief about that event, our interpretation of it. That is what prompts "C," the consequence: our emotional reaction.

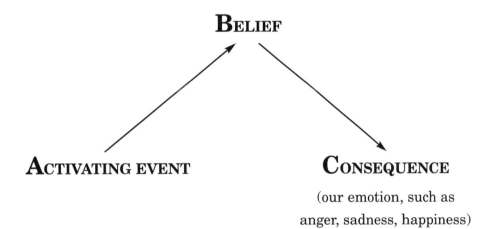

BELIEF

ACTIVATING EVENT

CONSEQUENCE
(our emotion, such as
anger, sadness, happiness)

For instance, it rains in Seattle.

You can interpret this event by thinking, "This just ruins my day. I hate it when it rains. Now the whole day is shot. I might as well go back to bed, I'm so depressed."

Or you can think: "Oh well, it's raining again. The reality is it rains in Seattle, and that's OK. I won't let the rain ruin my plans. I will adjust my plans and still have a good time."

Symptoms of Adolescent Depression

An adolescent is considered depressed if five or more of the following symptoms are present during the same two-week period, *and* they include at least one of the first two (in italics).

- *depressed mood most of the day, nearly every day, as indicated by feelings of sadness, emptiness, tearfulness*

- *markedly diminished interest or pleasure in most activities*

- irritable mood or agitation

- acting-out behavior (missing curfews, unusual defiance)

- change in appetite, either loss or an increase in appetite

- significant unintentional weight loss or weight gain

- insomnia (sleeplessness) or hypersomnia (sleeping more than normal)

- excessive daytime sleepiness

- extreme restlessness or slowness of movement

- low energy level, chronic fatigue

- feelings of worthlessness or self-hatred

- excessive or inappropriate guilt

- frequent difficulties in concentration or decision-making

- recurrent thoughts of death or suicide

- plans to commit suicide

Suicide Danger Signs

These are danger signs to look for if you suspect a friend is suicidal.

- direct suicide threats and comments, such as "I wish I was dead" or "You'd be better off without me"

- a previous suicide attempt, no matter how long ago

- preoccupation with death in music, art, and writing

- loss of a family member, pet, or boyfriend or girlfriend (through death, abandonment, or breakup)

- family disruptions (parental unemployment, serious illness, relocation, divorce)

- problems with sleeping, eating, and personal hygiene

- problems with schoolwork; loss of interest in activities that had been important

- dramatic changes in behavior patterns, such as a shy person suddenly becoming extremely outgoing

- prevailing sense of gloom, hopelessness, and helplessness

- withdrawal from family members and friends; alienation of important people

- giving away prized possessions

- a series of "accidents," increase in risk-taking, or loss of interest in personal safety

If you see a friend showing any of these behaviors, seek help immediately.

Remember, suicide is a permanent "solution" to a temporary problem, and there are many things that can be done to solve the problems that are making the person feel hopeless.

Inhalants

What is inhalant use, and how risky is it?

Inhalant use refers to the intentional breathing ("huffing") of gas, solvents, or chemical vapors to reach a high that lasts about 15 to 45 minutes. Inhalants are legal, every-day products such as spray paint, liquid correction fluid, hair spray, paint thinners, felt-tip markers, glues, acetone products, carburetor cleaner, and gasoline. But huffing is dangerous, both in the short and long term. "Sudden Sniffing Death" (SSD) is common: the huffer suffocates when all the oxygen in the lungs is replaced by the fumes. SSD can happen the first time, the tenth time, or the hundredth time. One in ten will not survive the first experience. A heart attack is also possible.

Slang terms: *Glue, kick, bang, sniff, huff, poppers, whippets*

What can I do if someone huffing is in a state of crisis?

Remain calm and seek help. Remove anything blocking the breath, such as a plastic bag. If the huffer has passed out, gently position them so they can breathe. (Agitation may make the huffer violent, hallucinate, or suffer heart dysfunction.) Avoid letting them inhale their own vomit, which is usually fatal. Make sure the room is well ventilated. Call EMS (emergency medical services). If the person is not breathing, administer CPR (cardiopulmonary resuscitation).

Symptoms of inhalant abuse include:

- red, runny nose, nosebleeds; chronic cough; sores on mouth and nose
- headaches, dilated pupils; difficulty concentrating; sudden memory loss
- slowing of body's functions; loss of coordination; nausea and vomiting
- spaced-out behavior; loss of consciousness

Long-term adverse effects:

- damage to brain, heart, liver, kidneys, blood, bone marrow, and other organs
- violent behavior, unconsciousness, heart failure, and even death
- brain cell death, resulting in personality changes, memory impairment, learning disabilities, loss of coordination, slurred speech, and tremors
- physical and psychological addiction; users suffer withdrawal symptoms
- numbing nerve damage to back and legs; lung damage from inhaling spray paint

Methamphetamine

"Meth" is a highly addictive synthetic stimulant. As a powder, it dissolves easily and can be swallowed, snorted, injected, or smoked. A crystallized form can also be smoked. Users get an intense rush of energy and euphoria that can last hours, followed by a devastating crash, often with cravings for more meth. That's what makes it so addictive. Meth is made in illegal "labs" out of toxic chemical ingredients, many of them readily available (battery acid, drain cleaner, and antifreeze, for example). Some users make it at home, turning their homes into poisonous, dangerous places. These lethal chemicals also increase users' risk of heart attack, stroke, and brain damage. Tolerance builds quickly, and the user needs more meth for the same effect. Withdrawal symptoms include depression, anxiety, and fatigue; intense cravings; paranoia and aggression.

Slang terms: *Speed, tweak, uppers, chalk, zip, amp. Crystal meth is also called crystal, ice, crank, and glass.*

Short-term effects:

- wakefulness; increased physical activity; low appetite
- fast breathing; hyperthermia (high fever)
- irritability and aggressiveness; tremors and convulsions

Ongoing effects can include:

- tolerance and addiction, accompanied by changes in the brain
- violent behavior; mood disturbances, anxiety, confusion, paranoia
- delusions; auditory hallucinations

Chronic (long-term) meth use can lead to:

- all the above symptoms, in more severe degrees
- insomnia (sleeplessness)
- various kinds of hallucinations, such as the sensation of crawling insects
- homicidal and suicidal thoughts; violent or psychotic behavior
- brain cell loss: damage to memory, information processing, and decision making
- body movement disorders; muscle spasms and twitches

Inhalants Worksheet

1. _____

2. _____

3. _____

4. _____

5. _____

6. _____

7. _____

8. _____

9. _____

10. _____

Methamphetamine Worksheet

1. _____

2. _____

3. _____

4. _____

5. _____

6. _____

7. _____

8. _____

9. _____

10. _____

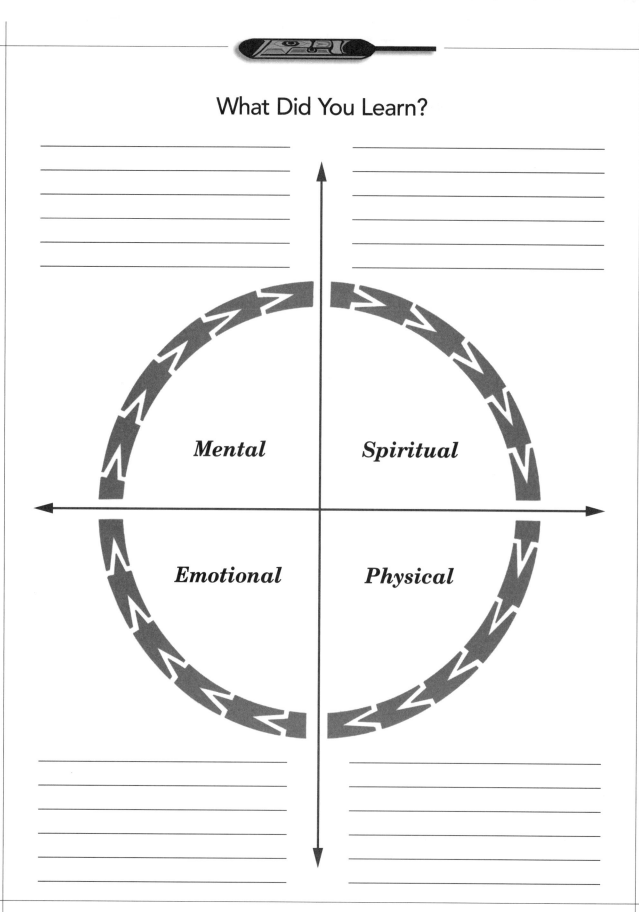

What Did You Learn?

Mental *Spiritual*

Emotional *Physical*

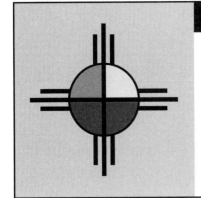

True Strength

EMPOWERING OUR BODY AND SPIRIT

Purpose of Session 8

In this session participants discuss ways to strengthen both body and spirit. They also see how alcohol and other drugs such as steroids and depressants can poison the body and spirit, as reflected in the story *Getting Hooked*—a story that also offers a message of hope. At the end of this session, optional handouts on preparing for the future are provided. Topics include resume writing, job interviewing, job productivity, stress management, and more; these can be distributed to participants as appropriate.

Learner Outcomes

By the end of this session, participants will be able to:

- discover the problems that drugs and alcohol can create

- explain how addiction can easily occur

- determine how expectations influence our perceptions

- identify the consequences of drug and alcohol use

Materials Needed

☐ flip chart, white board, or chalk board

☐ markers or chalk

☐ handout 8.1, *Steroids*

☐ handout 8.2, *Depressants*

☐ handout 8.3, *Steroids Worksheet* (one copy only)

☐ handout 8.4, *Depressants Worksheet* (one copy only)

☐ handout 8.5, *What Did You Learn?*

☐ optional: handouts 8.6–8.13. These offer practical work-related tips on these topics: *Steps to Writing an Effective Resume, Typical Questions to Expect in a Job Interview, Questions to Ask in a Job Interview, Acting Appropriately on the Job, Getting Ready to Start Your Job, Workplace Dating and Sexual Harassment, Increasing Job Productivity and Quality,* and *Ways to Cope with Stress.*

Preparation Needed

1. Read session 8 in its entirety to become familiar with it.

2. Practice reading aloud the story *Getting Hooked: Freddy the Flying Fish*, found in this session.

3. Photocopy the first five handouts and hole-punch if needed. Handouts appear in this book after each session outline; they can also be printed from the CD-ROM (if using a color printer, decorative elements will appear in color). During the session, distribute them one by one as prompted.

4. Optional: If appropriate, photocopy the remaining handouts with job-related tips, one for each participant. Or choose the relevant handouts on a case-by-case basis.

5. Arrange the room so that each participant can be included in the conversation.

6. If you created ground rules in session 1, post them for all participants to view.

"Getting Hooked": An Introduction to Addiction

In this section, participants hear and discuss a story about addiction. Through a flying fish named Freddy, the story depicts the lure of drugs. But it also shows that Freddy finds hope through the self-help school of fish called NA ("Neonaholics Anonymous").

Say:

In this session we'll talk about addiction, and how easily it can happen. We'll start with a story called *Getting Hooked: Freddy the Flying Fish*, written by Dr. Alan Marlatt.

Read aloud:

Getting Hooked: Freddy the Flying Fish
by Alan Marlatt, Ph.D.

Off the coast of southern California, not too far from Santa Catalina Island, a group of flying fish found their home. Among them lived Freddy, a teenage flying fish, who loved to shoot upwards through the water as fast as he could, breaking through the surface, gliding above the wave tops sparkling with sunbeams, and finally diving deep back into the ocean.

Unlike many of his fellow flying fish who resorted to flying only as means of escaping such predators as the deadly shark (who is too heavy to fly in pursuit of his prey), Freddy and a few of his friends liked to fly for the sheer pleasure of the experience. A few flying fish had even gone on to set speed and distance records at the Ocean Olympics at Atlantis, but Freddy did not aspire to this kind of competitive flying. He simply loved the exhilaration of breaking through the resistance of the water world into the light airiness above the surface. Unlike most fish who had no knowledge or experience of the air world above their heads, Freddy had direct experience with a higher level of awareness, one that existed just above the surface level. This special experience was something he had difficulty explaining to his friends who could not fly, such as Clara the Codfish or Tony the Tuna.

Freddy had two close friends. Frank the Flying Fish was a levelheaded, serious type who harbored ambitions to set up

Duplicating this page is illegal. Do not copy without publisher's written permission.

185

an accredited flying school. Another flying fish friend was Flipper, a school-of-fish dropout, who spent most of his time looking for new ways of getting high (mostly through sex, drugs, and rock and roll).

Freddy met his girlfriend, Francine, while they both were flying. One golden evening, just as the sun was sinking below the horizon, while Freddy soared above the waves in one of his longest flights ever, he glanced to his left just in time to see a beautiful young flying fish gliding gracefully by in the opposite direction. Their eyes met briefly as they flashed by, and Freddy felt warm sensations of romantic excitement as he dove back into the depths to seek her out. Freddy and Francine soon became boyfriend and girlfriend and spent more and more of their time together, frequently flying in tandem like two stones skipping over the sea from one wave crest to another. It was clear to both Frank and Flipper that Freddy and Francine were in love.

One day, after a particularly long and exciting flight with Francine, Freddy was approached by Flipper. Flipper was act-ing strangely—he was hyper, excited, and actually appeared to glow in luminescent colors as he spoke to Freddy. Frank and Francine swam by to join the conversation. As it turned out, Flipper was high from eating a neon fish, a little known fish that he discovered one day off the south coast of Santa Catalina Island.

"These neon fish are great!" Flipper raved. "They make you feel even better than when you're flying—better because you don't have to do any work, just swallow one neon fish and you'll feel high for hours! Come on, Freddy! I know where we can find some if we leave right away—the neon fish are just getting out of school about now. Let's split!" Francine, although saying nothing, looked upset, as it was obvious that Freddy was tempted.

Suddenly, Frank spoke up, his voice grave and concerned. "According to the teachings of Moby Dick, some neon fish have hooks in them—but there's no way of telling just by looking at them which ones have hooks in them and which ones do not. But if you bite into one with a hook—ZAP! You're a goner!

Many fish have disappeared from the face of the ocean after biting into a hook, and no one saw them again!"

There followed a long discussion concerning the risk of getting hooked. Flipper insisted that only about one out of every thousand neon fish actually contained a hook. Frank countered that the risk was much higher, that as many as one out of every ten neon fish had a hook in it. Francine said that it didn't seem worth the risk. "I only have one life," she exclaimed. "Why should I take the chance even if the odds were only one in a million? If I get the one with the hook, I'm dead!"

But it was no use. Freddy swam off with Flipper. Frank and Francine stayed behind. They both looked worried.

Freddy's first neon fish made him feel higher than he had ever felt before. Moments after swallowing his first bite, he felt a warm glow pulse throughout his body. Flipper laughed uproariously, and he saw Freddy turn a series of phosphorescent colors, first a deep ruby red, an electric blue, followed by a lingering golden glow. Not only is there no hook in this neon fish, Freddy exulted, but this feels <u>fantastic</u>! He felt powerful and masculine, even more so than when things were going great with Francine.

Most important to Freddy was the realization that the feelings he got from the neon fish were more exciting than those he experienced while flying. "I feel on top of the ocean!" he yelled to Flipper as they swam up behind a pair of unsuspecting neon fish. "And yet, here we are, many fathoms below the surface! It's wild!"

As the days passed into weeks and months, Freddy spent more and more of his time with Flipper. Together they sought out neon fish wherever they could find them. They both became increasingly preoccupied with neon fish, following them home each day after school, concerned that their supply might run out. Freddy spent less time with either Francine or Frank. Having gained weight from eating so many neon fish, both Flipper and Freddy became sluggish and slow in their swimming. Neither had flown above the surface in many weeks.

Francine finally decided to confront Freddy with her concerns. She told him that she thought he was addicted to the neon fish and that, if he didn't do something soon, he was likely to hit the bottom.

Freddy shuddered for a moment as he thought of the dangers of the murky ocean bottom—the sharks, the octopus, and the deadly manta ray, the devilfish himself. "Don't worry, Francine—there's no way I'm going to hit the bottom. I'm still myself—I'm alive, right? I've eaten many neon fish and not a single one had a hook inside! So how can I be hooked?" He grinned, trying to minimize the growing sense of guilt he felt whenever Francine or Frank tried to talk with him about his behavior. Francine swam away sadly.

A week later, something terrible happened to Flipper while he and Freddy were pursuing some neon fish to deeper and deeper levels. Just as Flipper was about to lunge at a particularly attractive purple and gold neon fish, a hammerhead shark appeared ominously nearby. The shark took after Flipper. "Watch out! SHARK!" Freddy screamed, but it was too late. Overweight and out of shape, Flipper could not build up enough speed to escape the shark. Just before hitting the surface of the ocean and flying off to freedom, Flipper was grabbed by the tail by the hammerhead and snatched under. Although he struggled desperately, it was over in an instant. Freddy watched in horror as the shark devoured his friend.

Flipper's death shocked Freddy into action. After Flipper's funeral, Freddy vowed to give up neon fish forever. He decided to seek help from others, turning to Frank and Francine for suggestions. Frank recommended that he spend three weeks in treatment in the Electric Eel Clinic, where they offered an aversion therapy program for neonaholism. Francine, on the other hand, suggested he attend a self-help school of fish called NA (Neonaholics Anonymous), made up of fish who were all recovering from the same addiction.

After several months of participation in both programs, Freddy committed himself to a lifelong period of total abstinence from all neon fish. He was told that because of his disease, he must avoid neon fish forever, that even so much as a tiny nibble of neon fish flesh would reactivate the disease. He was even told that neonaholism was an inherited, progressive disease and that there was no cure. All he could do was arrest the disease by staying away from all neon fish for the rest of his life.

After several weeks of abstinence, Freddy started to feel like his old self. He lost some weight and soon was able to fly again, just as in the old days. Francine and Freddy began dating again. They both spent a lot of time with Frank.

Three months later, Freddy had a slip. After a painful fight with Francine one night, Freddy was swimming home alone when he suddenly saw a lone neon fish, brilliantly glowing in green and orange a fathom below. At first he tried to ignore the temptation, but he found himself thinking the following thoughts: "I'm feeling angry with Francine. I know I would feel instantly better if I had a hit of neon fish. Surely just one can't hurt—after all, I never was really hooked before. I ate hundreds of neon fish and not a single one ever had a hook in it. Since no one is around, why not? Who would know? I think I'll swim a little deeper, drop down a level, just to get a better look at those flashing colors."

Freddy gobbled down the neon fish. He felt a mix of reactions—the spreading fire of the neon glow inside his belly (it felt particularly intense since he was no longer as tolerant to the effects), but coupled with a sense of guilt and failure. It's no use, Freddy thought—this just proves I have no willpower. Why should I try? I can't fight the disease. The more miserable he became, the greater became the lure of the neon fish as an instant relief. Soon he was back into his old addictive pattern, feeling both helpless and victimized. The neon fish became both the problem and the cure: the worse he felt, the more he was tempted to eat another neon fish to escape his bad feelings. The neon glow always felt good for a little while, but the long-range effects grew much more painful. His friends started to see less of him. Francine was particularly upset, but she did not know where to turn for help.

Finally Freddy could stand it no longer. There's no use," he thought. "I can't seem to live without neon fish; yet, I can't live with them either—look at what happened to Flipper. These things will kill me in the end. But what can I do?" Tired and at his wit's end, he finally decided to turn to Moby Dick for help. Although never a religious fish, Freddy opened his heart and asked for help from the Great White Whale. "I can't do it on my own," he cried. "Please help me."

That night, Freddy had a vision. He was visited by a beautiful white sailfish who said she swam all the way from Hawaii especially to see him. The sailfish seemed so real that Freddy was not sure if he was dreaming or awake. "My name is Sarah, Freddy. Come with me," she said warmly, taking Freddy by the fin. "We're going to fly higher than you have ever been before."

Freddy was amazed at how easy and effortless it was to swim alongside Sarah, who seemed to glow brighter the faster she swam. Their speed increased to an incredible velocity as they neared the surface of the water. When they at last broke through, the surface exploded like a mirror shattering into thousands of brilliant shards. Bursting through the crest of a huge wave, a tsunami wave triggered by an undersea earthquake somewhere near the Hawaiian Islands, Freddy experienced soaring through galaxies of stars in the midnight sky all around him. As the light of the huge golden moon glittered on the waves like diamonds, Freddy sailed between stars on the water and stars in the sky above. The Pacific waves surged below as Freddy and Sarah flew together in silence, buoyed up by the currents of the warm summer wind. They skipped off the wave tops as they sailed along, Sarah with her long white sail fins stretched out like the wings of an albatross.

After what seemed like an eternity, they dove back down into the warm ocean currents. Freddy felt totally exhilarated. His body was filled with a golden glow, warmer and more joyful than any he had experienced before, even after eating the finest neon fish. In contrast, the glow of the neon fish seemed dull and lusterless, compared with the brilliance of the glow he now experienced.

Sarah smiled. "Now you know how high you can go. And even though I was with you, you were flying on your own, and now you can do it anytime you wish. It's so much higher than you can ever get with the neon fish. But, you know, the poor neon fish doesn't know how to fly above the water. That's why Moby Dick gave them the luminescent glow so that they could experience the fire within, even though they never reach the surface. But you, Freddy, you can fly on your own, higher and better than any neon fish can take you. Rely upon yourself; you don't need a crutch. Just keep your heart to your own higher power within, and you'll find that there is no limit as to how high and far you can fly."

With those words, Sarah swam slowly off into the dark night waters, her body glowing as if from some inner light.

Freddy never saw Sarah again, but he never forgot that night of flying above and below the stars. He began to work on his own flying more and more, finding that he could improve upon his performance each time he practiced. Within a year, he entered some flying competitions and soon developed a reputation as a champion flier.

A year and a half after his experience with Sarah, Freddy won a gold medal at the Atlantis Olympic games for the longest, highest flight ever recorded for a California flying fish. Freddy and Francine were friends and lovers once more. Frank opened his own professional flying school, with Freddy as his co-partner.

One day, while Freddy and Frank were swimming home after a day of teaching new fish how to fly, they both spotted a very attractive neon fish, glowing in bright rainbow colors, next to some seaweed. "Look at that one, Freddy," said Frank. "Do you think it has a hook in it, Freddy?" Freddy smiled and looked at his friend. "Yes," Freddy said with quiet but firm conviction. "They all have hooks in them."

Getting Hooked is reprinted from Marlatt, G.A., and Fromme, K., "Metaphors for Addiction," *Journal of Drug Issues* 17 (1987), 9–28. Used with permission.

Ask:

So what lesson do we learn from Freddy the flying fish?

Allow for responses.

Duplicating this page is illegal. Do not copy without publisher's written permission.

191

The Choice Is Ours

Explain using your own words:

We have talked a lot about canoe journeys, who goes on them, how to get through rough waters, and so on. Now we are going to talk about what you take on your canoe journey.

Ask:

What are some things you would want to make sure you take with you on a canoe journey ?

Allow for responses and write them on the board or flip chart.

Ask:

Why is it important to take these things?

Allow for responses and write them on the board or flip chart.

Ask:

Are there things you would not want to take with you on a canoe journey? Why not?

Make a list of suggestions.

> ▶ **Facilitator Tip**
> To generate some lively conversation, you may suggest something silly like "a bowling ball" and observe that you don't really need it, it will just get in the way and make the canoe heavier to pull.

Alcohol and Other Drugs: Pros and Cons

This section reviews information on substance use and how it can impact a canoe journey—and a life journey. Participants explore both the pros and cons of taking drugs or alcohol on a canoe journey and a life journey.

Explain using your own words:

Now, of all the things we just talked about taking or not taking on our canoe journey, we are going to focus on two things in particular: drugs and alcohol.

There might be a lot of reasons why we do *not* want to take drugs or alcohol with us on a canoe trip *and* some reasons why we *would* want to.

On a flip chart or board, write "PROS" and "CONS" at the top of two columns.

PROS	CONS

Make sure participants understand that "pros" refer to the positives of the situation while "cons" refer to the negatives. Because this list will be used throughout Session 8, have it handy so you can add more pros and cons at any time.

Let's start with reasons *for* taking drugs or alcohol on the trip.

Ask:

What are some reasons why someone might want to take drugs or alcohol along on a canoe journey?

Write responses under "PROS."

Examples might include:
- We might feel more fearless at first
- We might feel able to stay up all night
- We might want to celebrate on the journey

Ask:

How about reasons for *not* taking drugs or alcohol on the canoe trip?

Write down responses under "cons." Examples might include:
- We might tip the canoe because of being reckless
- We might get sick and not be able to continue the journey

Explain using your own words:
Just as we have mentioned before, our canoe journey is a lot like our life journey. Some of these reasons for taking or not taking drugs or alcohol on our canoe journey might also apply to whether we want to have them along for our life journey.

Point out how some responses on the board might apply to life's journey.

Duplicating this page is illegal. Do not copy without publisher's written permission.

193

Ask:

Can you think of any other reasons we may or may not want to take drugs or alcohol on our life journey that are not already listed up here?

Allow for responses.

STEREOTYPES

"Stereotypes" could actually belong on both the Pro and Con lists. If it is not there already, add it to both lists. Then explain using your own words:

Some people might think that stereotypes are one reason to either use drugs or alcohol, or not use them.

Ask:

Do you know what a stereotype is?

Allow for responses.

Ask:

Does anyone know a stereotype about Native Americans and drinking?

Allow for responses.

Ask:

How do you think that stereotypes might either lead us to use or not use alcohol?

Allow for responses.

Explain using your own words:

We have come up with some factors that may affect the decision to use drugs or alcohol. Now we are going to talk about some other things that may affect this decision. They include:

- **possible consequences: health-related and others, including safety issues**
- **expectations**

Consequences

Explain using your own words:

Throughout these sessions, we've talked about the health consequences of drug and alcohol use—the effects on your physical health and mental health. Now let's talk about some other consequences.

We all know most drugs are illegal and that alcohol is illegal for people under 21. When people over 21 decide to drink, there are four areas that they most often have problems with.

Write these on the board or flip chart:

- motor vehicle accidents
- unsafe sex
- violence
- blackouts

If adults do decide to drink, how do you think they could prevent these problems from happening? For instance,

- **How would you prevent automobile accidents?**
- **How would you prevent unsafe sex from happening?**
- **How would you prevent violence from occurring while drinking?**

Generate a list for each problem.

Expectations

Explain using your own words:

"Expectations" is just a fancy word for what people expect to happen when they do something. There are certain things people expect to happen when they drink or do drugs. Expectations can be pretty powerful.

Ask:

What are some things that people expect to happen when they drink alcohol?

Possible suggestions might include:

- feel sexier or flirt better
- feel relaxed and less shy

- feel that they can have fun
- feel more feminine
- feel more masculine

Ask:

Do you think alcohol actually creates all of these feelings you mentioned?

Allow for responses.

Ask:

Do the chemicals in alcohol cause us to behave in the ways we've talked about?

Allow for responses.

Expectations of Alcohol: A "Balanced Placebo" Experiment

Explain using your own words:

Dr. Alan Marlatt, who is the director of the Addictive Behaviors Research Center at the University of Washington, conducted a study that looked at expectations. He and his group of researchers developed an experiment to test what kinds of effects alcohol really has on people.

Draw a two-by-two box on the board or on a flip chart. You will fill in the boxes when describing the experiment.

Explain using your own words:

First of all, what is a placebo?

Allow for responses.

If necessary, offer this definition:

In an experiment to test the effects of a substance, a placebo is a "lookalike" substance—an inactive substitute that is used with some of the subjects. The subjects don't know whether they have the "real" substance or the placebo. It helps experimenters sort out the real effects versus the perceived or expected effects.

In this experiment, subjects had one of four experiences:

- **They expected to drink alcohol but actually received a placebo (a nonalcoholic tonic drink that appears to be an alcoholic beverage).**
- **They expected to drink tonic water but actually received alcohol.**
- **They expected alcohol and received alcohol.**
- **They expected to drink tonic water and received tonic water.**

Explain using your own words:

By watching how the four groups responded, the chemical effects and the effects of psychological expectations can be separated.

Add these headings to each of the boxes above.

1. Expects alcohol and receives alcohol	2. Expects tonic and receives tonic
3. Expects tonic and receives alcohol	4. Expects alcohol and receives tonic

RESULTS OF THE RESEARCH

Ask:

How do you think the participants in each of the conditions acted? In particular, how do you think the participants responded in the two conditions where they received something different from what they were expecting?

Allow for responses and then provide the answers given below:

1. **What about the subjects who expected to receive alcohol and did receive alcohol? They acted pretty much the way we would think they might act. The subjects became more talkative, louder, and more flirtatious with each other.**

2. **The subjects who received tonic water and knew it was tonic water also acted pretty much the way you would think.**

The interesting results come from the other two groups:

3. **The subjects who received only tonic water but expected alcohol acted much like the group who expected alcohol and received it. They actually seemed to become louder, more verbal, and more flirtatious.**

4. **The subjects who received alcohol and thought they were only drinking tonic water did not act like this at all. They generally reported feeling tired and did not appear more social or talkative.**

Ask:

What do you make of this? Did you expect that people who weren't drinking alcohol and were told that they were drinking alcohol would act the way they did?

Allow for responses.

Explain using your own words:
This just shows how powerful expectations are!

Steroids and Depressants

Explain:
Alcohol is one type of depressant. But there are others too, many in pill form. Another group of drugs we'll talk about are steroids. So let's form two groups for another relay race. One group will look at facts about depressants, and the other will look at steroids.

HANDOUT 8.1

HANDOUT 8.2

HANDOUT 8.3

HANDOUT 8.4

Form two groups and, if needed, ask them to sit together.

Pass out handout 8.1, "Steroids," to the first group and handout 8.2, "Depressants," to the second group.

Then give the first group one copy of handout 8.3, and the second group one copy of handout 8.4. They will use these worksheets to answer your questions, one at a time.

Explain to all participants:

I will give each group one question at a time. The group will find the correct answer on their handout, write the answer down, and pass it to me. I'll tell them if the answer is right, and if it is, the group can go on to the next question. If it's wrong, the group tries again. The two groups will be working at the same time. The team that answers all the questions correctly in the fastest time will win the relay.

> **Facilitator Tip**
> See pages 200–201 for the questions you will ask and the answers to expect. You can either ask the questions out loud (one at a time), or write them down in advance on slips of paper and hand them in sequence to each group.

After the relay race, discuss any questions or issues that came up.

Then ask:

Would we want to take steroids or depressants on a canoe journey?

Allow for responses.

Explain using your own words:

So that leads to the question that each of us should ask ourselves, "Do I want steroids or depressants to be a part of my life's journey?"

Facilitator Q and A: Steroids	
QUESTIONS	**ANSWERS**
1. For women, what are the signs of masculinization?	Signs include more body and facial hair, lower voice, irregular menstrual periods, and skin problems.
2. For men, what are the signs of feminization?	Signs include breast enlargement, testicular shrinkage, fatty deposits, soft muscles, balding, and lower natural testosterone production.
3. What two methods are used for taking steroids?	Ingesting in pill form and injecting under the skin.
4. Why is "more is better" a false notion when it comes to steroids?	Only tiny amounts are needed to be effective. For medical purposes, doctors prescribe them in doses of 1 to 5 milligrams a day.
5. How can high doses of steroids damage bones?	They can damage the growth areas at the ends of the bones, permanently stunting growth.
6. How can high doses of steroids affect moods?	They can cause mood swings, depression and irritability, delusions, impaired judgment, and combativeness.
7. What is "roid rage"?	Aggression and combativeness triggered by use of steroids.
8. How do steroids act on individual cells in the body?	They enter the nucleus of the cell and alter the genetic material to stimulate the production of new proteins.
9. Why do people use steroids?	Some people use them as a shortcut to build muscle and improve body performance and appearance—in the short term.
10. How could steroid use put a person at risk for HIV infection?	If people share needles used to inject steroids, they can also transfer HIV this way.

Facilitator Q and A: Depressants	
QUESTIONS	**ANSWERS**
1. How do depressants affect the central nervous system?	They slow it down.
2. What are some symptoms of withdrawal from depressants?	Chills, cramps, muscle tremors, insomnia, and anxiety,
3. If you suddenly stop taking high doses of depressants, what could occur?	Possible convulsions, delirium, and even death.
4. Why are depressants prescribed medically?	To relieve anxiety, irritability, and tension.
5. What are some slang terms for barbituates?	Downers, goofballs, blues, and barbs.
6. What are the effects of moderate doses of depressants?	Mild intoxication, impaired judgment and perception, confusion, slurred speech, release of inhibitions.
7. What are two possible outcomes of an overdose of depressants?	Coma and death.
8. What are some slang terms for methaqualone?	Soapers, quads, ludes.
9. If a person develops a tolerance to depressants, what two kinds of dependence can result?	Physical and psychological.
10. How addictive are depressants?	Highly addictive.

Conclusion

HANDOUT 8.5

Here we summarize what has been learned throughout this session using the Medicine Wheel.

Give each participant a copy of handout 8.5, "What Did You Learn?"

Draw a Medicine Wheel on the board.

Ask:

Using the Medicine Wheel's four dimensions, what could we say that we have learned in this session?

Allow for responses. Possible answers might include:

Mental

- I have learned about how different drugs, including alcohol, can affect me.
- I have learned that expectations influence what I think about drinking alcohol.

Spiritual

- I have learned how drugs and alcohol can hinder my effort to be successful on my life journey.
- I have learned that in order to honor the Creator I must stay away from substances that harm my mind and body.

Emotional

- I have learned how drugs and alcohol affect me emotionally.
- I now pay more attention to the ways I am pressured to use.
- I have learned that drug use affects my emotions.

Physical

- I have learned how substances affect my body physically
- I have learned that I do not honor my body by using harmful substances.

Ask each participant to share an item or two from the handout. Ask questions to spark discussion.

> ▶ **Facilitator Tip**
> Participants should be given time to complete the handout
> during the session. Do not allow participants to take the
> assignments home.

OPTIONAL MATERIAL

Handouts on Work-Related Activities for Life's Journey

Preparing for the Future

Share eight extra handouts on job interviewing, job productivity, resume writing, and related topics. They can be given to individual participants as appropriate. Or, if they are relevant to the whole group, briefly review all the handouts and then ask participants to use them for future reference.

> ▶ **Facilitator tip**
> You may want to emphasize that these handouts are helpful
> when applying for a job and preparing for the questions a future
> employer might ask.

Explain in your own words:

Although we are almost through with the life skills sessions, I would like to give you one more set of handouts. These will be useful to you as you prepare for adult life. Some of the topics include writing a resume, preparing for questions in a job interview, preparing for a job, coping with stress, and so on.

Duplicating this page is illegal. Do not copy without publisher's written permission.

203

OPTIONAL HANDOUTS

Distribute the handouts and briefly describe the content. If you have time, review each handout.

HANDOUT 8.6

HANDOUT 8.7

HANDOUT 8.8

HANDOUT 8.9

HANDOUT 8.10

HANDOUT 8.11

HANDOUT 8.12

HANDOUT 8.13

Program Conclusion

Explain in your own words:

This is the conclusion of the *Canoe Journey—Life's Journey* sessions. We have covered a lot of information and discussed many skills that may help you in your journey through life.

Ask:

In review, what are some of the things that you have learned in these sessions?

Allow for responses. List may include:

- learning from the Medicine Wheel
- learning from the canoe journey

- self-awareness
- spiritual and traditional lessons
- connection to the community
- setting goals
- problem solving
- decision making
- communication skills
- effective listening
- assertiveness
- coping with negative emotions
- anger management
- conflict resolution
- stress reduction
- making decisions about alcohol and other drugs
- maintaining good health
- preparing for the future

After the participants have come up with a list, review the possible answers listed above and suggest any they might have missed.

Explain in your own words:

We have really enjoyed having this time with you. We have presented a great deal of material and we hope that you will be able to use some of these skills in the future.

Have a safe journey!

Duplicating this page is illegal. Do not copy without publisher's written permission.

205

Steroids

What are steroids, and how are they used?

Anabolic steroids are synthetically made from the male hormone testosterone. They may be medically prescribed, but some people unwisely take them as a shortcut to build muscle and boost athletic performance—in the short term. Steroids help the body retain protein: they go straight into organ and muscle cells and alter the genetic material to stimulate the production of new proteins. Steroids are either taken as pills or injected into the muscle. A tiny dose is effective. A typical doctor-prescribed daily dose is about 1 to 5 milligrams, but under the false notion that more is better, some abusers take megadoses of hundreds of milligrams.

Slang terms: *Gym candy, pumpers, A's, stackers, anabolics, bolins, anabols, balls or bulls, weight trainers, Arnolds, Arnies, dep-testosterone, roids, methyltestosterone, juice*

Risks of steroid abuse
- damage to growth areas at the end of bones, permanently stunting growth
- weakened tendons, resulting in tearing or rupture
- headaches related to hormonal imbalance
- high blood pressure, hardening of arteries, heart palpitations or attack, stroke
- liver damage, which can lead to cancer, jaundice, bleeding, and hepatitis
- impaired kidney function; possible kidney stones and disease
- risk of HIV infection through sharing injection needles
- mood swings, depression, irritability, delusions and impaired judgment
- uncontrolled aggression and combativeness ("roid rage")
- withdrawal symptoms that intensify the psychological effects

What about gender-related side effects?

High doses over time produce other adverse effects. For women, masculinization occurs: more hair on body and face, lower voice, irregular menstrual periods, and skin problems with enlarged pores and severe acne. For men, feminization occurs as excess testosterone changes into the female hormone estrogen: breast enlargement, testicular shrinkage, tendency toward fatty deposits, very soft muscles, balding, and lower natural production of testosterone.

Depressants

What are depressants?

Some depressants are legal; they are prescribed medically to relieve anxiety, irritability, and tension. Others are illegal: their users are after a high that is similar to alcohol intoxication. Depressants slow down the central nervous system. Tolerance and dependence, both physical and psychological, can build quickly. Many depressants are highly addictive; methaqualone and barbituates are two of these types. After long-term use, suddenly stopping or reducing a high dose may cause convulsions, delirium, and even death. Other withdrawal symptoms can include insomnia and anxiety, chills and cramps, and muscle tremors.

Slang terms: Methaqualone: *Soapers, quads, ludes*

Barbituates: *Downers, goofballs, blues, barbs*

What are the effects of depressants?

Low-dose effects:

- calmness; relaxed muscles; sense of well-being
- slight dizziness; impaired coordination
- mild impairment of thought

Moderate-dose effects (more pronounced):

- mild intoxication; release of inhibitions
- clouded judgment; impaired perception; confusion
- slurred speech

High-dose effects (more intense and unpredictable):

- babbling, impaired thinking and memory; distorted sense of reality
- staggering, stumbling; lack of coordination; reduced sex drive
- difficulty concentrating; confusion; slow reactions
- weak control of emotions; depression; paranoia; hostility; risk of suicide

Other physical effects include:

- lower breathing rate, heart rate, and blood pressure; sleepiness
- clammy skin; dilated pupils
- possible coma or death from overdose

Steroids Worksheet

1. _____

2. _____

3. _____

4. _____

5. _____

6. _____

7. _____

8. _____

9. _____

10. _____

Depressants Worksheet

1. _____

2. _____

3. _____

4. _____

5. _____

6. _____

7. _____

8. _____

9. _____

10. _____

What Did You Learn?

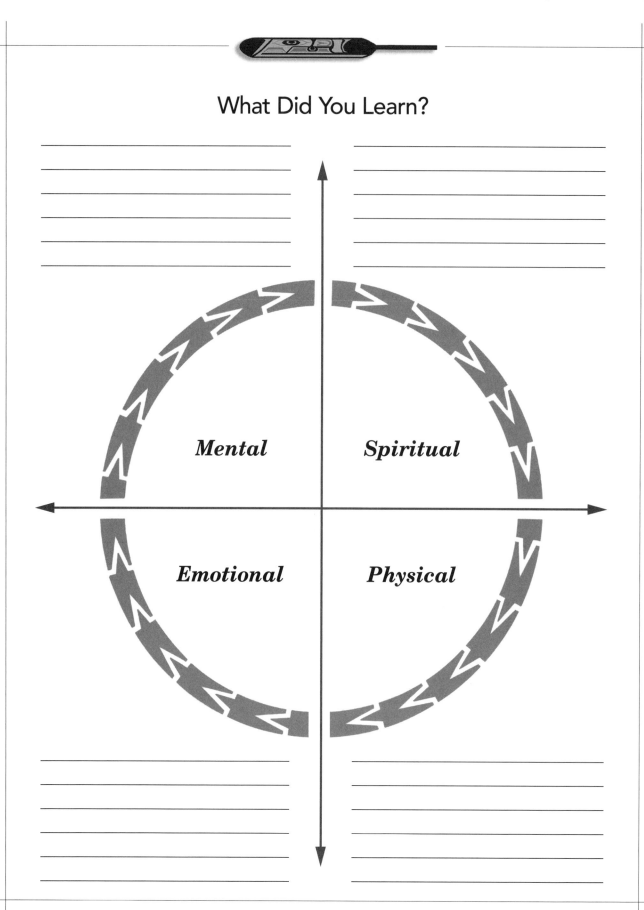

Mental   Spiritual

Emotional   Physical

Steps to Writing an Effective Resume

Do a self-assessment

First ask yourself: What are my skills and abilities? What is my work experience? Outside of the academic classes I took in school, what activities have I done? (These are also called extracurricular activities.)

Gather your contact information

All contact information should go at the top of your resume. This includes name, address, telephone number, and e-mail address.

- Avoid nicknames

- If possible, use a permanent address and telephone number. Use your parent/guardian's or a friend's. Include the area code.

Define an objective

An objective tells people about the sort of work you want to do. Be specific and feel free to change it to fit the job you are seeking. For example:

- Objective: Seek a retail sales position utilizing my customer service experience.

- Objective: Gain experience in the restaurant and food service industry.

Decide what to include

List your work experience, community service, education (include honors or GPA if it is impressive), special skills (for instance, computer programs or musical talents), participation in sports or clubs, and any leadership positions you've held. Tips for listing work experience:

- Use action words to describe your job duties.

- List jobs in reverse chronological order (most recent job first).

- Include position title, name of organization, dates of employment, and description of work responsibilities, with emphasis on skills and achievements.

How should it look?

Use white or off-white 8½ x 11-inch single-sided paper. Type it and use simple fonts, nothing decorative, 10 to 14 points in size. Make sure you have no spelling or grammatical errors.

Typical Questions to Expect in a Job Interview

Listed here are common questions and possible answers.

1. *How did you hear about the job?*
    Mention a friend, relative, classified ad, newspaper story—any details showing that your interest in the company isn't random.

2. *Why do you want this particular job?*
    Talk about the interesting aspects of the job and why you are drawn to them.

3. *What skills does this job require?*
    Use your fingers and count off the skills: one ... two ... three. . .

4. *What qualifications do you have?*
    Using your fingers, name a skill and list your qualifications. Then move on to the next skill.

5. *Tell me about my company.*
    Before the interview, look the company up on the Internet or call the local chamber of commerce. Get information on the company size, its key products or services, the markets where it competes, and its general reputation.

6. *Why do you want to work for us?*
    You're on your own for this one. Have a good answer ready.

7. *Relax and tell me about yourself.*
    Talk about your experience, qualifications, and accomplishments—not your childhood, family, or hobbies.

8. *How many other employers have you approached?*
    You might say, "Several for backup, but this is where I really want to work. This is where my hopes are."

9. *How many employers have you worked for during the last five years?*
    Tell the truth.

CONTINUED ON NEXT PAGE

10. *You seem to switch jobs a lot. Why?*
Some possible reasons: These jobs were not challenging enough, the company downsized, I needed to do some career exploration, I had a short-lived personal problem, I made a bad choice.

11. *How long do you plan to work here?*
You might say, "A long time. This is the job I've been hoping for."

12. *Are you prepared to work overtime?*
You might say, "Yes, I'm willing to put in as many hours as it takes to get the job done," or maybe "Yes, I am willing to occasionally work overtime." The interviewer may place high importance on this if the job requires it.

13. *What have you learned or gained from your previous work experience?*
Use your fingers and list the various skills you have learned and knowledge gained.

14. *Tell me about your current (or last) job.*
List your duties and responsibilities. Explain your accomplishments.

15. *Why are you leaving your current (or last) job?*
Possible reasons: job stagnation, demotion due to downsizing, career exploration, or simply having made a bad choice.

16. *Are you planning to give notice if you decide to leave for another job?*
Explain that you don't want to leave them short-handed. A two-week notice is customary.

17. *What will your manager say when you give notice you're leaving?*
Explain why you'll be missed. Don't give the impression that they'll be glad to be rid of you.

18. *What did you like most about your current (or last) job?*
Talk about your responsibilities, challenges, accomplishments, and the people.

19. *What would you change about that job?*
Don't bad-mouth the job. Explain that you'd want more responsibilities. It shows initiative.

20. *Did you ever have a disagreement with a boss? Why? Why not?*
Answer "yes" and you're a troublemaker, "no" and you're a wimp. Find the middle ground: "Sure, we disagreed. But we worked well together. For example . . ."

CONTINUED ON NEXT PAGE

21. *Tell me about your education or training.*
    Explain your education or training and tell how it helped prepare you for this job.

22. *Did you enjoy school? Why?*
    The manager may want to know if you enjoy learning and whether you might benefit from a training program.

23. *Which course did you find most difficult? Why?*
    The manager wants to know if you have perseverance. You might say something like, "I got a D in my first term in algebra. My study skills were all wrong. I joined a study group. By third term I pulled it up to a B and kept it there."

24. *Did you join any school activities? Why?*
    School activities show that you're sociable, that you enjoy being part of a group, and that you can work with other people. This is important in the workplace. If you didn't join any activities, explain that you needed to study or work, but you enjoy being with people.

25. *How were your grades in math?*
    The job may require basic math skills: addition, subtraction, multiplication, division, and percentages. You might answer, "I had a problem with calculus, but my basic math skills are good."

26. *How were your grades in English?*
    The job may require reading. It may also require you to write reports. Give an honest answer.

27. *Do you plan to continue your education?*
    Continuing education courses suggest growth, ambition, and promotability. In some workplaces you might qualify for tuition assistance.

28. *What do you do to relax after work?*
    Don't brag about car racing, skydiving, scuba diving, or other dangerous sports. They suggest a likelihood of injury and absence from work.

29. *What do you plan to be doing for work five years from today?*
    In advance, figure out the promotions you should get if you work hard for this employer over the next five years. Tell the manager you plan to be working for him or her in that position.

30. *What do you think you can do well at in this job?*
    Talk about parts of the job where your personal strengths will come in handy.

CONTINUED ON NEXT PAGE

31. *Give an example of any major problem you faced and how you solved it.*
Think of something related to work, school, civic, or leisure activities.
Tell it as a story. Give details. The manager wants to see how you define
a problem, identify options, decide on a solution, handle obstacles, and
solve the problem.

32. *In your lifetime, what was your greatest accomplishment? What did you learn
from it?*
A personal touch works well here, such as a family-related accomplishment, or helping someone in need.

33. *What was your greatest failure? What did you learn from it?*
Fessing up to a failure shows maturity. Avoid examples that might
reflect on your ability to do the job.

34. *What is your greatest weakness?*
Focus on work, not character weaknesses. Turn it into a positive: "I'm
accused of being a workaholic. I like to stay and get caught up on the
odds and ends before I go home."

35. *Have you ever been convicted of a crime?*
It's legal to ask this question if it has a bearing on the job you are seeking. A bank, for example, wouldn't want a convicted embezzler working
in the vault. If you have a conviction, admit it. Explain what happened.
Admit that you made a stupid mistake. Tell what you've done to make
amends. Ask for a second chance.

36. *Do you have a drug or alcohol problem?*
If you answer "yes" to this question, get some help. Enroll in a program.

37. *Last year, how many days of work (or school) did you miss? How many days
were you late?*
This will tell the manager whether you're going to show up for work on
time every day. If you've missed more than a couple of days, have some
good explanations ready.

38. *What motivates you to do a good job?*
"Money" is not a good answer. Instead, say something like "Having
responsibilities and being acknowledged when the job is done right."

39. *Are you at your best when working alone or in a group?*
"Both. I enjoy working as part of a team and I can work independently to
get my share of the work done."

CONTINUED ON NEXT PAGE

40. *What would you do if a supervisor told you to do something now, and another supervisor told you to do it later?*
The manager wants to see how you would handle conflict. How would you handle it?

41. *Give me two reasons why I should* not *hire you.*
You're on your own, but be ready for this question.

42. *Who are your heroes? Why?*
Think about it in advance!

43. *What do you like most about yourself? Least?*
Use your fingers and stress your positives.

44. *If you were told to report to a supervisor who was a woman, belonged to a minority group, or was physically disabled, what problems would this cause for you?*
You're on your own.

45. *What salary were you paid in your last job?*
Tell the truth.

46. *What kind of salary are you looking for today?*
"I have no set salary. What salary is usually offered to someone with my qualifications?" If the manager persists, give a general answer such as "Somewhere in the teens" or "Somewhere in the thirties."

47. *In your last job, how much overtime did you average each week?*
The manager wants to know if you can be counted on to help out when the work mounts. Explain that you can be counted on to work late whenever the need arises.

48. *Have you ever been fired from a job? Why?*
Explain that you usually get along really well with everyone. But you and your ex-manager just couldn't seem to make things work.

Questions to Ask in a Job Interview

You should always have some questions ready to ask the prospective employer. It shows that you have taken an interest in the company.

Note: Do not ask all these questions; just pick a few that you like.

1. If hired, would I be filling a newly created position, or replacing someone?

2. Was the last person who had this job promoted?

3. Could you describe a typical workday and the things I'd be doing?

4. Which duties are most important for this job? Least important?

5. How would I be trained or introduced to the job?

6. How long should it take me to get my feet on the ground and become productive?

7. How is the job important to the company—how does it contribute?

8. Who are the people I'd be working with, and what do they do?

9. Can someone in this job be promoted? If so, to what position?

10. How would I get feedback on my job performance, if hired?

11. If hired, would I report directly to you, or to someone else?

12. If you were to offer me this job, where could I expect to be in five years?

13. What do you consider to be my weaknesses? Strengths?

14. Could you give me a brief tour? I'd enjoy seeing where your people work.

15. What could I say or do to convince you to offer me this job?

Acting Appropriately on the Job

Always be considerate of others. When talking, use a conversational tone of voice. Talking loudly or obnoxiously can be disruptive to other workers and customers. You can have fun and be more relaxed during breaks, but always maintain self-control from the time you arrive at work until you go home. Avoid pranks and jokes that can disrupt the work environment or disturb customers or other workers. For example, it is OK to put a funny cartoon on someone's desk, but do not dismantle someone's chair so it breaks when they sit in it.

Watch your language. Using curse words, calling people names, or using other insulting words can be offensive to others. Using slang may make good communication difficult between co-workers and customers. Slang is going to vary from person to person and time period to time period. For example, a 60-year-old may not understand "That shirt is fresh." A 20-year-old would probably understand it to mean the shirt is good looking.

When dealing with customers, do not do silly or weird things for your co-workers' entertainment. For example, do not tell a customer jokingly, "If you need any help, do not bother me. I do not get paid enough." This kind of banter is risky—and all it takes is one complaint to get you into trouble with the boss. Use good manners when working with customers. Answer questions appropriately and politely ("Yes, ma'am," "No, sir"), ask another worker if you cannot help a customer, and in general try to be as helpful as possible.

Getting Ready to Start Your Job

Use this checklist as you prepare for your first day on the job.
Call the personnel coordinator and get the appropriate information.

- What time should I arrive?
- Where should I report, and who should I ask for?
- Do I need to bring any of the following forms? (Check the ones needed.)

    ___ identification document (birth certificate, driver's license, picture ID)

    ___ Social Security card

    ___ work permit (if you are under 18)

    ___ occupational license (if needed)

    ___ valid, unexpired Employment Authorization Card (if you are an immigrant)

    ___ medical records (physical exam report, doctor's authorization to work)

- What special equipment do I need?
- What do people usually do for lunch?
- Do I need a uniform? Yes___ No___

    If yes:
    - Do I need it on the first day?
    - What do I need, and where do I find it?
    - How many should I get?
    - What is the cost? Do I pay up front, or is it taken out of my paycheck?

    If no:
- What should I wear?

    Find out what to wear, then check at home. Do you have appropriate clothing? Is it clean, in good condition, and durable enough for the job? Do you have enough to last between washes? If you can't answer yes to all of these questions, consider buying new clothes. First decide how much you can spend, then make a list of the clothes you'll need. Check for sales, and consider thrift stores. Comparison shop for the best value.

Workplace Dating and Sexual Harassment

Dating in the workplace

Many people meet their future spouses at work. However, it is wise to follow these guidelines on dating in the workplace.

- Learn the company policy regarding dating in the workplace.

- If you ask someone out and you are turned down, take no for an answer. Repeatedly asking someone out could constitute sexual harassment.

- If you are dating someone at work, do not display affection at work. Kissing, hugging, and so on, is inappropriate (even in the janitor's closet).

- Keep in mind two potential major problems with dating a co-worker: First, being together both on and off duty can strain a relationship. No matter how much you like a person, everyone needs a break from one another. Second, a breakup can be very uncomfortable in the workplace

Sexual harassment

How to avoid sexually harassing a co-worker:

- If you are a supervisor, do not engage in any relationship with co-workers other than professional ones.

- Handshakes are OK. Any other physical touch could be considered harassment.

- If someone tells you that you did something that bothered them, stop doing it.

- Do not use offensive language, tell dirty jokes, or bring sexually charged items to work (porn magazines, gag gifts, lingerie, and so on).

What to do if you feel you are being sexually harassed:

- Tell the harasser to stop. Use your assertive communication skills. Say, "I do not think that is appropriate behavior for the workplace. Please stop."

- Keep a written record of what the harasser has done. Tell people close to you about what is going on.

- Learn your workplace's sexual harassment policy. Follow the procedure exactly as written. If the harasser does not stop, you may have to talk to that person's supervisor.

- If you have followed the company's procedure on stopping sexual harassment and it still has not stopped, contact a lawyer.

Increasing Job Productivity and Quality

Do the task the way your boss instructs you to do it.

Ask questions in the beginning. It takes less time to get additional instruction than to do the job over.

Make a schedule of what you have to complete.

Get all the materials ready to complete the task.

Start the job soon after receiving instructions. Taking it easy for 15 minutes prior to starting can make it difficult to get the job completed on time.

Do the job right. Review your work to see if there are any mistakes.

Correct mistakes as soon as possible. This will save time in the long run.

Make sure all parts of the job are complete. Even if you do 90 percent of the job perfectly, the 10 percent not completed will overshadow the good work you did.

Do the complete job as fast as possible.

When you have finished, move on to the next task. If you don't know what the next task is, ask. Don't just wait for someone to tell you.

Ways to Cope with Stress

Pay attention to your body and behavior. If you see signs of stress, look for coping strategies.

Avoid stressful situations if you can. For example, you cannot avoid job interviews, but you can try to stay out of debt and avoid problems with the law.

Rest and get plenty of sleep.

Use relaxation techniques to control breathing and reduce muscle tension.

Identify the cause of stress. Take action to change stressors that you can change. Accept what cannot be changed.

Manage time. Work on completing one task at a time.

Think positively.

Express feelings appropriately.

Be flexible and willing to make changes.

Do something fun. Read a book or do something to take your mind off the stressor.

References and Resources

In compiling this guidebook the authors used these resources, listed here topically. Suggested Internet resources follow.

Canoe Journeys

Neel, D. *The Great Canoes: Reviving a Northwest Coast Tradition.* Seattle: University of Washington Press, 1995.

Neel, D. "A Journey's End: The Commonwealth Games." *Native People's Magazine* 9(1)(1995): 26–32.

Community-Based Interventions

Edwards, E.D., Seaman, J.R., Drews, J., and Edwards, M.E. "A Community Approach for Native American Drug and Alcohol Prevention Programs: A Logic Model Framework." *Alcoholism Treatment Quarterly* 13(2)(1995): 43–62.

Fleming, C.M. "The Blue Bay Healing Center: Community Development and Healing as Prevention" (monograph). *American Indian and Alaska Native Mental Health Research* 4(1994): 135–165.

Indian Health Service & Center for Substance Abuse Prevention. *Gathering of Native Americans (GONA) Facilitator Guide.* Rockville, MD: Substance Abuse and Mental Health Services Administration, Center for Substance Abuse Prevention, 1999.

Lefley, H.P. "Self-perception and Primary Prevention for American Indians." In S.M. Manson (ed.), *New Directions in Prevention Among American Indian and Alaska Native Communities* (65–89). Portland, OR: Oregon Health Sciences University, 1982.

Wallerstein, N. and Bernstein, E. "Empowerment Education: Freire's Ideas Adapted to Health Education." *Health Education Quarterly* 15(4)(1988): 379–394.

Watts, L.K. and Gutierres, S.E. "A Native American–Based Cultural Model of Substance Dependency and Recovery." *Human Organization* 56(1)(1997): 9–18.

Cultural Sensitivity

Atwood, M.D. *Spirit Healing: Native American Magic and Medicine.* New York: Sterling Publishing, 1991.

Dinges, N.G., Trimble, J.E., Manson, S.M., and Pasquale, F.L. "Counseling and Psychotherapy with American Indians and Alaska Natives." In A.J. Marsella and P.B. Pedersen (eds.), *Cross-cultural Counseling and Psychotherapy* (243–276). New York: Pergamon, 1981.

Kessel, J. "Working with Indian Adolescents." In C. Baker (ed.), *Working with Adolescents: The Changing Scene.* Ann Arbor: National Child Welfare Training Center, University of Michigan, 1982.

LaFromboise, T.D. and Low, K.G. "American Indian Children and Adolescents." In J.T. Gibbs, L.N. Huang and Associates (eds.), *Children of Color* (114–147). San Francisco: Jossey-Bass, 1989.

LaFromboise, T.D., Trimble, J.E., and Mohatt, G.V. "Counseling Interventions and American Indian Tradition: An Integrative Approach." *Counseling Psychologist* 18(4)(1990): 628–654.

Northwest Child Welfare Training Institute. *Heritage and Helping: A Model Curriculum for Indian Child Welfare Practice.* Module 3. Portland, OR: Indian Foster Family Care, 1984.

Reimer, C.S. *Counseling the Inupiat Eskimo.* Westport, CT: Greenwood Press, Contributions to Psychology, no. 36, 1999.

Emotions, Moods, and Mindfulness

Linehan, M. *Skills Training Manual for Treating Borderline Personality Disorder.* New York: Guilford Press, 1993.

Life Skills/Refusal Skills

Bobo, J.K. "Preventing Drug Abuse Among American Indian Adolescents." In L.D. Gilchrist and S.P. Schinke (eds.), *Preventing Social and Health Problems through Life Skills Training,* 43–54. Seattle: University of Washington, 1985.

Bobo, J.K., Snow, W. H., Gilchrist, L.D., and Schinke, S.P. "Assessment of Refusal Skills in Minority Youth." *Psychological Reports* 57:3 (part 2) (1985), 1187–1191.

Botvin, G.J. "Substance Abuse Prevention Through Life Skills Training." In R.D. Peters and R.J. McMahon (eds.), *Preventing Childhood Disorders, Substance Abuse, and Delinquency* (215–240). Thousand Oaks, CA: Sage Publications, 1996.

Brochu, S. and Souliere, M. "Long-term Evaluation of a Life Skills Approach for Alcohol and Drug Abuse Prevention." *Journal of Drug Education* 18(4)(1988): 311–331.

LaFromboise, T.D. *American Indian Life Skills Development Curriculum.* Madison, WI: University of Wisconsin Press, 1996.

Schinke, S.P. and Cole, K.C. "Methodological Issues in Conducting Alcohol Abuse Prevention Research in Ethnic Communities." In P.A. Langton (ed.), *The Challenge of Participatory Research: Preventing Alcohol-Related Problems in Ethnic Communities* (129–147). Rockville, MD: Center for Substance Abuse Prevention, DHHS Publication No. (SMA) 95-3042, 1995.

Medicine Wheel/Four Directions

Allen, P.G. *The Sacred Hoop.* Boston: Beacon Press, 1986.

Bopp, J., Bopp, M., Brown, L., and Lane, P. *The Sacred Tree.* 3rd ed. Lethbridge, Alberta, Canada: Four Worlds Development Press, 1989.

Garrett, J. T. "Indian Health: Values, Beliefs, and Practices." In Harper, M.S. (ed.), *Minority Aging: Essential Curricula Content for Selected Health and Allied Health Professions* (179–191). Washington, D.C.: Health Resources & Services Administration, Department of Health and Human Services, DHHS Publication No. HRS (P-DV-90-4), U.S. Government Printing Office, 1990.

Hodgson, M. "The Nechi Institute on Alcohol and Drug Education." In M.O. Nielsen and R.A. Silverman (eds.), *Native Americans, Crime, and Justice* (271–277). Boulder, CO: Westview Press, 1996. Reprinted from *Canadian Woman Studies* 10(2/3)(1990): 101–104.

Thurman, P.J., Swaim, R., and Plested, B. "Intervention and Treatment of Ethnic Minority Substance Abusers." In J.F. Aponte, R.Y. Rivers, and J. Wohl (eds.), *Psychological Interventions and Cultural Diversity* (215–233). Needham Heights, MA: Allyn & Bacon, 1995.

Peer Support

Carpenter, R.A., Lyons, C.A., and Miller, W.R. "Peer-Managed Self-control Program for Prevention of Alcohol Abuse in American Indian High School Students." *International Journal of the Addictions* (20)(1985): 299–310.

Lyons, C.A., Carpenter, R.A., and Strelich, T.J. *The Intermountain Model: An American Indian Peer-Assisted Alcohol Abuse Prevention Program.* Brigham City, UT: Bureau of Indian Affairs, Office of Technical Assistance and Training, 1982.

Oetting, E.R. and Beauvais, F. "Peer Cluster Theory: Drugs and the Adolescent." *Journal of Counseling and Development* 65(1)(1986): 17–22.

Topping, K. "Reaching Where Adults Cannot: Peer Education and Peer Counseling." *Educational Psychology in Practice* 11(4)(1996): 23–29.

Prevention

Moran, J.R. and May, P.A. "American Indians," in J. Philleo and F.L. Brisbane (eds.), *Cultural Competence for Social Workers* (3–39). Rockville, MD: Center for Substance Abuse Prevention, Vol. 4, CSAP Cultural Competence Series, DHHS Publication No. (SMA) 95-3075, 1995.

Spirituality

Hall, R.L. "Distribution of the Sweat Lodge in Alcohol Treatment Programs." *Current Anthropology* 26(1)(1985): 134–135.

Levy, J.E., Neutra, R., and Parker, D. *Hand Trembling, Frenzy Witchcraft, and Moth Madness.* Tucson: University of Arizona Press, 1987.

Mails, T.E. *Dog Soldiers, Bear Man and Buffalo Woman: A Study of the Societies and Cults of the Plains Indians.* Englewood Cliffs, NJ: Rutledge/Prentice-Hall, 1973. (A discussion of Lakota secret societies and spirituality.)

Navarro, J., Wilson, S., Berger, L.R., and Taylor, T. "Substance Abuse and Spirituality: A Program for Native American Students." *American Journal of Health Behavior* 21(1)(1997): 3–11.

Walters, A.L., Beck, P.V., and Francisco, N. (1990). *Sacred: Ways of Knowledge, Sources of Life.* Flagstaff, AZ: Northland Press. (Earlier edition published in 1977 by Navajo Community College, Tsaile, AZ.)

Storytelling

Marlatt, G.A. and Fromme, K. "Metaphors for Addiction." In S. Peele (ed.), *Visions of Addiction* (1–24). Lexington, MA: Lexington Books, 1988.

Strange Owl, R. (1984). "Doing a Trick with Eyeballs." In R. Erdoes and A. Ortoz (eds.), *American Indian Myths and Legends* (379–381). New York: Pantheon. (Told by Rachel Strange Owl in Birney, Montana in 1971 and recorded by Richard Erdoes.)

Tafoya, T. "Unmasking Dashkayak: Storytelling and HIV Prevention." *American Indian Alaska Native Mental Health Research* 9(2)(2000): 53–65.

Substance Use and Abuse

Brindis, C., Berkowitz, G., Peterson, S., and Snider, S. *Evaluating the Effectiveness of Alcohol and Substance Abuse Services for American Indian / Alaska Native Women.* Phase 2, Final Report. Rockville, MD: Indian Health Service, 1995.

Cortes, D.E., ed. *Cultural Issues in Substance Abuse Treatment.* Rockville, MD: Center for Substance Abuse Treatment, DHHS Publication No. (SMA) 99–3278, 1999.

Dorpat, Norm. "PRIDE: Substance Abuse Education/Intervention Program" (monograph). *American Indian and Alaska Native Mental Health Research* 4(1994): 122–133.

Herring, R.D. "Substance Abuse Among Native American Youth: A Selected Review of Causality." *Journal of Counseling and Development* 72(6)(1994): 578–584.

Robbins, M.L. "Native American Perspectives." In J.U. Gordon (ed.), *Managing Multiculturalism Substance Abuse Services* (148–176). Thousand Oaks, CA: Sage Publications, 1994.

Other References

Choney, S.K., Berryhill-Paapke, E., and Robbins, R.R. "The Acculturation of American Indians." In J.G. Ponterotto, J.M. Casas, L.A. Suzuki, and C.M. Alexander (eds.), *Handbook of Multicultural Counseling* (73–92). Thousand Oaks, CA: Sage Publications, 1995.

Ferguson, F.N. "Navajo Drinking: Some Tentative Hypotheses." *Human Organization* 27(1968): 159–167.

LaLonde, M. *A New Perspective on the Health of Canadians.* Ottawa, Canada: Canadian Ministry of Health and Welfare, 1974.

McFee, M. "The 150% Man: A Product of Blackfeet Acculturation." *American Anthropologist* 70(1964): 1096–1107.

Reader's Digest Editors. "Northern Worlds: The Arctic, Subartic, and Northwest Coast." In Cobbs, Flowers, Gardner, and Loomis (eds.), *Through Indian Eyes: The Untold Story of Native American People* (234–255). Pleasantville, NY: Reader's Digest, 1999.

Duplicating this page is illegal. Do not copy without publisher's written permission.

227

Suggested Internet Resources

Medicine Wheel

What Is a Medicine Wheel?
http://users.ap.net/~chenae/spirit.html

Journeying the Medicine Wheel
www.carmel.com/scott/medicinewheel-in03.html

Alcohol and Drugs

Alcohol

General Facts
www.freevibe.com/Drug_Facts/alcohol.asp

"The Cool Spot": Alcohol and Resisting Peer Pressure
www.thecoolspot.gov/

Tips for Teens: The Truth About Alcohol
http://ncadi.samhsa.gov/govpubs/ph323/

Club Drugs

General Facts
www.nida.nih.gov/drugpages/clubdrugs.html

Tips for Teens: The Truth About Club Drugs
http://ncadi.samhsa.gov/govpubs/phd852/

GHB
www.freevibe.com/Drug_Facts/ghb.asp

Ketamine
www.freevibe.com/Drug_Facts/ketamine.asp

Rohypnol
www.freevibe.com/Drug_Facts/rohypnol.asp

Hallucinogens

General Facts
www.freevibe.com/Drug_Facts/hallucinogens.asp

Tips for Teens: The Truth About Hallucinogens
http://ncadi.samhsa.gov/govpubs/phd642/

LSD
www.nida.nih.gov/drugpages/acidLSD.html

PCP (Phencyclidine)
www.nida.nih.gov/drugpages/pcp.html

Inhalants

General Facts
www.nida.nih.gov/drugpages/inhalants.html
www.freevibe.com/Drug_Facts/inhalants.asp

Ask Dr. NIDA—Inhalants
http://teens.drugabuse.gov/drnida/drnida_inhale1.asp

NIDA for Teens—Inhalants
http://teens.drugabuse.gov/facts/facts_inhale1.asp

Tips for Teens: The Truth About Inhalants
http://ncadi.samhsa.gov/govpubs/phd631/

Marijuana

General Facts
www.nida.nih.gov/drugpages/marijuana.html
www.freevibe.com/Drug_Facts/marijuana.asp

Ask Dr. NIDA—Marijuana
http://teens.drugabuse.gov/drnida/drnida_mj1.asp

NIDA for Teens—Marijuana
http://teens.drugabuse.gov/facts/facts_mj1.asp

Tips for Teens: The Truth About Marijuana

> http://ncadi.samhsa.gov/govpubs/phd641/

Nicotine and Smoking

General Facts

> www.nida.nih.gov/drugpages/nicotine.html
> www.freevibe.com/Drug_Facts/smoking.asp

Ask Dr. NIDA—Nicotine

> http://teens.drugabuse.gov/drnida/drnida_nic1.asp

NIDA for Teens—Nicotine

> http://teens.drugabuse.gov/facts/facts_nicotine1.asp

Prescription Medication Abuse

General Facts

> www.drugabuse.gov/drugpages/prescription.html
> www.freevibe.com/Drug_Facts/prescription_drugs.asp

NIDA InfoFacts: Prescription Pain and Other Medications

> www.nida.nih.gov/Infofacts/PainMed.html

Steroids

General Facts

> www.nida.nih.gov/drugpages/steroids.html
> www.freevibe.com/Drug_Facts/steroids.asp

Ask Dr. NIDA—Anabolic Steroids

> http://teens.drugabuse.gov/drnida/drnida_ster1.asp

NIDA for Teens—Anabolic Steroids

> http://teens.drugabuse.gov/facts/facts_ster1.asp

Tips for Teens: The Truth About Steroids

> http://ncadi.samhsa.gov/govpubs/phd726/

Stimulants

Ask Dr. NIDA—Stimulants

> http://teens.drugabuse.gov/drnida/drnida_stim1.asp

Mind Over Matter—Stimulants

> http://teens.drugabuse.gov/mom/mom_stim1.asp

NIDA for Teens—Stimulants

> http://teens.drugabuse.gov/facts/facts_stim1.asp

Cocaine

> www.freevibe.com/Drug_Facts/crack.asp
> www.nida.nih.gov/Infofacts/cocaine.html

Ecstasy

> www.freevibe.com/Drug_Facts/ecstasy.asp

Heroin (discussed in curriculum as an opiate)

> www.nida.nih.gov/Infofacts/heroin.html
> http://ncadi.samhsa.gov/govpubs/PHD861/
> www.freevibe.com/Drug_Facts/heroin.asp

Methamphetamine

> www.nida.nih.gov/drugpages/methamphetamine.html
> www.freevibe.com/Drug_Facts/meth.asp

Hazelden Foundation, a national nonprofit organization founded in 1949, helps people reclaim their lives from the disease of addiction. Built on decades of knowledge and experience, Hazelden's comprehensive approach to addiction addresses the full range of individual, family, and professional needs, including addiction treatment and continuing care services for youth and adults, publishing, research, higher learning, public education, and advocacy.

A life of recovery is lived "one day at a time." Hazelden publications, both educational and inspirational, support and strengthen lifelong recovery. In 1954, Hazelden published *Twenty-Four Hours a Day,* the first daily meditation book for recovering alcoholics, and Hazelden continues to publish works to inspire and guide individuals in treatment and recovery, and their loved ones. Professionals who work to prevent and treat addiction also turn to Hazelden for evidence-based curricula, informational materials, and videos for use in schools, treatment programs, and correctional programs.

Through published works, Hazelden extends the reach of hope, encouragement, help, and support to individuals, families, and communities affected by addiction and related issues.

For questions about Hazelden publications, please call 800-328-9000 or visit us online at hazelden.org/bookstore.

Hazelden DVDs that may interest you

Youth Life Skills DVD collection (ages 14–18)

This series presents powerful peer-to-peer messages about problem solving and living responsibly. In their own words, real teens explain how they handled difficult situations in the past and what they learned from their experiences. Topics: *Anger Management, Communication, Conflict Resolution, Decision Making,* and *Stress Management.* Five 10-minute DVDs, each with a printable facilitator guide on CD-ROM.

ORDER NO. 2685

Steps One, Two, and Three for Adolescents (ages 14–20)

Admitting to powerlessness, coming to believe, turning over one's will—a teen's experience of the first three Steps of Twelve Step recovery can differ dramatically from an adult's. Sarah, Adam, and other teens share their triumphs and setbacks in candid, heartfelt stories about parents, school, and friendships. Three 12-minute DVDs with discussion guides.

ORDER NO. 7960

Sobering Facts: The Risks of Alcohol Use (ages 12–18)

Alcohol use is so pervasive in our society that, sooner or later, every teen will face personal decisions about underage drinking. With a strength-based approach and an emphasis on making safe decisions, *Sobering Facts* equips teens with important information about alcohol use, how it affects the brain, how it increases the likelihood of accidents and injuries, and how it can harm school performance, relationships, and health. DVD, 11 minutes.

ORDER NO. 2576

To order call **1-800-328-9000** or visit
www.hazelden.org/bookstore.